FLIRT

Anita Blake, Vampire Hunter, novels

GUILTY PLEASURES

THE LAUGHING CORPSE

CIRCUS OF THE DAMNED

THE LUNATIC CAFE

BLOODY BONES

THE KILLING DANCE

BURNT OFFERINGS

BLUE MOON

OBSIDIAN BUTTERFLY

NARCISSUS IN CHAINS

CERULEAN SINS

INCUBUS DREAMS

MICAH and STRANGE CANDY

DANSE MACABRE

THE HARLEQUIN

BLOOD NOIR

SKIN TRADE

FLIRT

LAURELL K. HAMILTON

FLIRT

AN ANITA BLAKE,
VAMPIRE HUNTER, NOVEL

headline

First published in the United States of America in 2010 by
The Penguin Group (USA) Inc.
A BERKLEY BOOK

First published in Great Britain in 2010 by
HEADLINE PUBLISHING GROUP

1

ISBN 978 0 7553 7435 9 (Hardback)
ISBN 978 0 7553 7436 6 (Trade paperback)

Typeset in Monotype Fournier by Ellipsis Books Limited, Glasgow

Printed and bound in Great Britain by
Clays Ltd, St Ives plc

Headline's policy is to use papers that are natural, renewable and
recyclable products and made from wood grown in sustainable forests.
The logging and manufacturing processes are expected to conform to
the environmental regulations of the country of origin.

HEADLINE PUBLISHING GROUP
An Hachette UK Company
338 Euston Road
London NW1 3BH

www.headline.co.uk
www.hachette.co.uk

This one's for Daven and Wendi,
friends who finally taught me the fine art of flirting.
Thanks for the inspiration.

For Jonathon, too, because he was there by my side
when inspiration struck. He has taught me that to be happy
with someone, first they must be my friend.
Without that there can be nothing else.

ACKNOWLEDGMENTS

To Carri, who, with this book, saw the process from beginning to end for the very first time. Welcome aboard. Shawn, Semper Fi. I know you both have my back. Pili, thanks for the food and the friendship. To the rest of the crew who are still hanging in there: Mary, Sherry, and Teresa. To Jennie, for all the funny and the hard work. To my writing group: Tom Drennan, Deborah Millitello, Marella Sands, Sharon Shinn, and Mark Sumner.

INTRODUCTION

HOW DO I get my ideas? How do I know it's enough for a book? How do I work?

I get these questions so often that when the idea for this book, *Flirt*, came to me, I decided to pay attention to the entire process from initial idea to finished product. You can read the novel and then read the nonfiction piece at the end of this book that tells the real-life event that inspired *Flirt*.

And once you've read the book and essay, you'll get cartoons. No, really – cartoons from Jennie Breeden of 'The Devil's Panties.' The comics are her take on the event that inspired it all. If you read the essay or peek at the cartoons you will spoil some of the surprise of the novel. So, no peeking, okay? Think of it as a spoiler alert. You have been warned.

Now turn the page and enjoy spending some quality time with Anita Blake.

'I WANT YOU to raise my wife from the dead, Ms Blake,' Tony Bennington said, in a voice that matched the expensive suit and the flash of the Rolex on his right wrist. It probably meant he was a lefty. Not that his handedness mattered, but you learn to notice primary hands when people try to kill you on a semiregular basis.

'My condolences,' I said automatically, because Bennington didn't display any grief. His face was composed, almost blank, so that if he was handsome in that gray-haired, I'm-over-fifty-but-keep-in-good-shape way, the lack of expression took all the fun out of it. Maybe the blankness was his way of showing grief, but his gray eyes were steady and cold as they met mine. It was either some steely control of grief, or he didn't feel anything about his wife's death; that would be interesting. 'Why do you want me to raise your wife from the dead, Mr Bennington?'

'At the rates you charge, does it matter?' he asked.

I gave him a long blink and crossed my legs, smoothing the skirt over my thighs as automatically as I'd said my condolences. I gave him the edge of a smile that I knew didn't reach my eyes. 'It does, to me.'

An emotion filled his eyes then: anger. His voice held barely a hint of the emotion that turned his eyes a darker shade of gray. Maybe it was steely self-control after all. 'It's personal, and you don't need to know it to raise her as a zombie.'

'This is my job, Mr Bennington, not yours. You don't know what I need to raise a zombie.'

'I did my research, Ms Blake. My wife wasn't murdered, so she won't rise as a vengeful, flesh-eating monster. She wasn't psychic, or a witch, and had never gone near any other religion that might make her more than a normal zombie. There's nothing in her background that makes her a bad candidate for the ceremony.'

I raised an eyebrow. 'I'm impressed; you did do your research.'

He nodded, once, manicured hands smoothing his tailored lapel. 'Then you'll do it?'

I shook my head. 'Not without a reason.'

He frowned at me, that flash of anger back in his eyes. 'What kind of reason do you want?'

'One good enough to make me disturb the dead.'

'I'm willing to pay your rather exorbitant fee, Ms Blake; I would think that would inspire you.'

'Money isn't everything, Mr Bennington. Why do you want her raised from the dead? What do you hope to gain from it?'

'Gain,' he said. 'I don't know what you mean by that.'

'I don't, either, but you keep not answering my original question; I thought maybe if I rephrased it you would.'

'I don't want to answer either question,' he said.

'Then I won't raise your wife. There are other animators

at Animators Inc. who will be happy to take your money, and they don't charge my rates.'

'Everyone says you are the best.'

I shrugged. I was never sure what to say to things like that, and found silence worked best.

'They say you are a true necromancer and have power over all types of undead.'

I kept my face blank, which I'd gotten better at over the years. He was right, but I didn't think it was commonly known. 'You'll turn a girl's head with talk like that.'

'You have the highest number of executions of any member of the US Marshals preternatural branch. Most of them were rogue vampires, but some of them were wereanimals.'

I shrugged. 'That's a matter of record, so yeah, but it has no bearing on what you want from me, Mr Bennington.'

'I suppose it has as little to do with my request as your reputation as a sort of female Casanova.'

'My love life really has nothing to do with my ability to raise the dead.'

'If you can truly control all manner of undead, then it might explain how you can slay vampires and still date them.'

Jean-Claude, one of the vampires in question, was a little iffy on who wore the pants in our relationship sometimes because of my powers; just as I was iffy on how much of our relationship was my idea because of his vampire powers over me. We had a sort of metaphysical detente. 'Jean-Claude and I were in the papers recently, so that didn't take much research.'

'One of St Louis's hottest couples, I believe was mentioned in the article.'

I tried not to squirm with embarrassment, and managed it. 'Jean-Claude is pretty enough that anyone on his arm looks hot.'

'That much modesty doesn't become a woman,' Bennington said.

I blinked at him, frowning. 'Sorry, I don't know what you mean by that.'

He studied my face, then said, 'You really don't, do you?'

'I just said that.' I felt like I had missed something, and didn't like it. 'I am sorry for your pain, but you're not winning me over.'

'I need to know if your reputation is real, or just talk, like so many of the tall tales about you.'

'I've earned my reputation, but if you really did your research on me then you also know that I don't raise zombies for kicks, or thrill seekers, or tormented relatives unless they have a plan.'

'A plan. What kind of plan?'

'You tell me. Why – do – you – want – your – wife – raised – as – a – zombie?'

'I understood the question, Ms Blake; you don't have to say it slowly.'

'Then answer the question, or this interview is over.'

He glared at me, that anger darkening his eyes to a nice storm-cloud gray. His hands made fists on the chair arms, and a muscle in his jaw flexed as he ground his teeth in frustration. Iron self-control it was.

I stood up, smoothing my skirt down in back, out of habit. I'd been polite because I knew how much money he'd paid just to talk to me, and since I was going to refuse I wanted him to feel he'd gotten something for his money, but I'd had enough.

'I need you because there isn't much left of her body. Most animators need a nearly intact body to do the job; I don't have an intact body to work with.' He wouldn't look at me as he said it, and there was a flinching around his mouth, a tension to those eyes he was hiding from me. Here was the pain.

I sat back down and my voice was gentler. 'How did she die?'

'It was an explosion. Our vacation home had a gas leak. She'd gone up ahead of me. I was going to join her the next day, but that night . . .' His fists tightened, mottling the skin, and that muscle in his jaw bulged as if he were trying to bite through something hard and bitter. 'I loved my wife, Ms Blake.' He sounded like the words choked him. His dark gray eyes gleamed when he raised them back to me. He held on to his unshed tears the way he held on to everything else: tightly.

'I believe you, and I really am sorry for your loss, but I need to know what you think you'll get out of raising her like this. She will be a zombie. Mine look very human, Mr Bennington, very human, but they aren't. I don't want you to believe that I can raise her up and you can keep her with you, because you can't.'

'Why can't I?'

I made my voice soft as I told him the truth. 'Because eventually she'll start to rot, and you don't want that to be your last visual of your wife.'

'I heard you raise zombies that don't even know they're dead.'

'Not at first,' I said, 'but eventually the magic wears off, and it's . . . not pretty, Mr Bennington.'

'Please,' he said, 'no one else can do this but you.'

'If I could raise her from the dead for real for you, maybe I would. I won't debate the whole religious/philosophical problem with you, but the truth is that even I can't do what you want. I raise zombies, Mr Bennington, and that is not the same thing as resurrection of the dead. I'm good, maybe the best there is in the business, but I'm not that good. No one is.'

A tear began to slide down each cheek, and I knew from my own hatred of crying that the tears were hot, and his throat hurt with holding it all in. 'I don't beg, Ms Blake – ever – but I'll beg you now. I'll double your fee. I'll do whatever it takes for you to do this for me.'

That he was willing to double my fee meant he had as much money as he seemed to have; a lot of people who wore designer suits and Rolex watches were wearing their money. I stood again. 'I am sorry, but I don't have the ability to do what you want. No one on this earth can bring your wife back from the dead in the way you want.'

'It's too late for her to be a vampire, then?'

'First, she'd have to have been bitten before she died to have any chance of raising her as a vampire. Second, you say she died in an explosion.'

He nodded, his face ignoring the tears, except for the pain in his eyes and the hard line of his jaw.

'Fire is one of the few things that destroy everything, even the preternatural.'

'One of the reasons I'm here, Ms Blake, is that most

animators have trouble raising the dead when there're just burned bits left. I thought that was because of how little they had to work with, but is it because of the fire itself?'

It was a good question, an intelligent question, but I didn't have a good answer to give back to him. 'I'm honestly not sure. I know that most animators need a nearly complete body to raise from the dead, but I'm not sure I've ever seen an article on whether death by fire impedes the process.' I stood up and walked around the desk to offer him my hand. 'I am sorry that I can't help you, Mr Bennington, but trust me that what I could do for you, you don't really want.'

He didn't stand up, just looked at me. 'You're the girlfriend of the Master Vampire of St Louis. Isn't he powerful enough to overcome all that and raise her as a vampire?'

I was a lot more than just Jean-Claude's girlfriend. I was his human servant, but we tried to keep that out of the media. The police that I worked with as a US Marshal already mistrusted me because I was having sex with a vampire; if they were certain of our mystical connection they'd like it even less.

I lowered my hand and tried to explain. 'I'm sorry, truly, but the Master of the City is still bound by some of the same laws of metaphysics as all vampires. Your wife would have to have been bitten several times before death, and the explosion would have destroyed her even if she had been a vampire.'

I put my hand back out and hoped he'd take it this time.

He stood up then, and shook my hand. He held on to my hand and gave me serious eye contact. 'You could raise her as a zombie that wouldn't know it was dead, and wouldn't look dead.'

I didn't pull my hand back, but let him hold it, though I didn't like it. I never liked being touched by strangers. 'I could, but in a few days she'd begin to deteriorate. If her mind went first then she'd just stop being your wife, but if the body began to rot before the mind went, then she'd be trapped in a decaying body, and she'd know it.' I put my hand over both of ours. 'You don't want that for her, or for yourself.'

He let go of my hand then, and stepped back. His eyes were lost rather than angry. 'But a few days to say goodbye, a few days to be with her, might be worth it.'

I almost asked if by 'be with her' he meant sex, but I did not want to know. I didn't need to know because I wasn't raising this zombie. There had been cases of other animators raising deceased spouses and having that happen, which is why most of us make the client understand that the zombie goes back in the grave the same night it comes out. It avoided a whole host of problems if you just put the dead person back in its grave immediately. Problems that made me have to fight off visuals I did not need in my head. I'd seen way too many zombies to think sex was ever a good idea with the shambling dead.

I walked him to the door, and he came, no longer arguing with me. I wasn't sure I'd actually won the argument. In fact, I would bet he'd try to find someone else to raise his wife from the dead. There were a couple of animators in the United States who could do it, but they would probably refuse on the same grounds I had. The creep factor was entirely too high.

The door opened and he went through. Normally, that would have meant I could close the door and be done with him, but I caught a glimpse of someone who made me smile in spite of my client's grief. But then again, I'd learned a long time ago that if I bled for every broken heart in my office, I'd have bled to death from other people's wounds long ago.

Nathaniel had his back to us, and in the overlarge tank top with those boy-cut sleeves, a lot of muscle showed. His auburn hair was tied in a thick braid that traced down almost every inch of his five-foot, seven-inch frame. The braid trailed over wide, muscular shoulders down that back, to the narrow waist, and the tight rise of his ass, to fall down the muscled length of his thighs, calves, until the end of his braid stopped just short of his ankles. He had the longest hair of anyone I'd ever dated. His hair was darker than normal, still damp from the shower that he'd caught between dance class and picking me up for lunch. I tried to look reasonably intelligent before he turned around, because if just seeing him from behind made me stupid-faced, the front view was better.

It was Jason who peeked out from around Nathaniel's wider shoulders to grin at me. He had that look in his eyes, that mischievous look that said he was going to push his luck in some way. There was no malice to Jason, just an overly developed sense of fun. I gave him the frown that should have told him, *Don't do anything that I'll regret.* It did no good to say he would regret it, because he wouldn't.

He was handsome, too, but he, like me, was not the prettiest person in the room with Nathaniel standing there. He was Nathaniel's best friend, and I lived with the prettiest boy in the room, so we were used to it. What made Jason appealing was not the packaging – the blue eyes; the yellow-blond hair, now long enough that he'd started having Nathaniel French-braid it for dance class; the almost-not-there tank tops and shorts, which showed off his own muscular and very nice body, all packed into a nice five-foot, four-inch frame – it was that grin and that light of mischief that made his eyes bright with thinking naughty thoughts. Not sex, though that was in there, but just a host of things he knew he shouldn't do, but so wanted to do.

To forestall whatever he had planned, I said, 'I'm sorry for your loss, Mr Bennington, and sorry I can't help you more.'

Jason's a good guy at heart, and his face sobered, and I knew he'd take the hint. Nathaniel turned at the sound of my voice, but his face was sober, too. He knew what kind of work I did, and knew that I dealt with more grieving relatives than most police.

I had a moment to see those huge violet eyes, like an Easter surprise in a face that was somewhere between beautiful and handsome. I could never decide if it was the eyes or all that hair, then he'd pull the hair back so you could see his face. I'd gazed at him sleeping often enough to know that he was just that beautiful.

Bennington stopped right outside the door, looking at the two men. 'Aren't you going to introduce me?' He was climbing back into his blank face, all that anger and disappointment shoved down behind the iron of his will.

I wasn't, actually. 'Maybe they're not mine to introduce,' I said.

Bennington looked back at Nathaniel and Jason. 'You're dancers at Guilty Pleasures. The website says you're a wereleopard and a werewolf. My wife went on a shapeshifter night. She said it was extraordinary watching you slip your skin and change shape.'

I sighed and said, 'Mr Bennington, this is Brandon and Ripley.' I used their stage names automatically, because once someone recognizes someone from the club, it's just safer to continue to be that persona. All the dancers had their share of overzealous fans. It was doubly problematic when they were one of the shapeshifters who danced. Hate crimes are alive and well. Hell, there are still some western states where varmint laws cover wereanimals, so you can kill one and all you have to say is they attacked you, and get a blood test to prove that the dead human body was a lycanthrope of some kind. Nathaniel was also my leopard to call, and Jason my wolf to call. Through Jean-Claude's vampire marks and my own necromancy, I'd become a sort of living vampire with some of the powers of a master. Jean-Claude was descended from Belle Morte's line of vampires. They fed on love and lust as well as blood, and I'd inherited the need to feed through sex and love. If I didn't feed periodically I began to die. I might have been stubborn enough and embarrassed enough to simply let it happen, but long before I died Nathaniel would die, drained to death by his 'master,' and Damian, my vampire servant, would die, and then Jason. Suicide was selfish enough, but that would have been ridiculous. I was still making peace with the metaphysical mess my life had become.

Once upon a time I'd have sensed their beasts through the office door, but I was getting more control and so were they, so it was like with normal folks. They could surprise me if they wanted to.

Jason, aka Ripley, smiled, and it filled his face with that cheerful, hail-fellow-well-met that he could turn on and off. 'I don't remember seeing you at the club, Mr Bennington.'

'I haven't been, but as I said my wife visited you once or twice.' He hesitated, then got his phone out of the inside pocket of his suit coat. It was one of those phones with the big screen so you could watch video on it, if you didn't mind having the picture be the size of your palm. Bennington pushed some buttons and held the phone out to Jason. 'Do you remember her?'

Jason smiled, but shook his head. 'It must have been on a night I wasn't working. I'd have remembered her.'

Bennington held it out to Nathaniel. He didn't touch the phone, but looked at it, face solemn. He shook his head. 'She's very beautiful.'

'Was, Brandon, was beautiful.' He held the phone out to me. The woman was blond, and beautiful in that Hollywood way, so that she was truly beautiful but there was nothing to make her stand out from a dozen other blond beauties. It was a type of attractiveness that always seemed artificial, as if they were all made at the same factory and sent out into the world to seduce and marry well.

Nathaniel said, 'I'm sorry.'

'Why are you sorry?' he asked, and that flash of anger was back.

'Anita said she was sorry for your loss; isn't your wife who you lost?'

Bennington nodded.

'Then I am sorry.' I knew Nathaniel well enough to know that his emotion was a little stronger than just normal condolences, but I'd ask later when Tony Bennington was far away.

I was still trying to usher him out, but I had one last boyfriend outside the door. Micah had been planning to join us for lunch, if he could, and there he was, joining us. He stepped in, my height with brown hair that curled past his shoulders, tied back in a ponytail that had too many curls to make his hair lie flat. His eyes were green and yellow, and not human. That beautiful face – and for Micah it truly was beauty, not handsome, more delicate jawline, more slender – was only just masculine. The leopard eyes in that lovely face just added to the impact. He wore sunglasses most of the time to hide the eyes. He started to get the glasses out automatically when he glimpsed the man behind me.

'Don't bother hiding the eyes,' Bennington said, 'I saw the interview you did for the news. You're the head of the Coalition for Better Understanding Between Humans and Lycanthropes, and I know you're a wereleopard.'

Micah stopped trying to fish his glasses out of his suit jacket pocket and just stepped in with a smile. 'I believe if we keep hiding what we are, it just adds to the fear factor.' He didn't offer his hand, because some humans didn't want to touch any part of you once they knew you were a shapeshifter. Bennington put his hand out, and Micah took it.

'Tony Bennington, this is Micah Callahan,' I said.

They shook hands just like normal folks. It got Bennington a brownie point.

'Again, Mr Bennington, I am sorry that I can't help you, but I urge you not to try to find someone else to raise your wife.'

'It's my money; I can find someone who will take it.'

'Yes, but no one will be able to give you back your wife. Trust me; a zombie is not the same thing, Mr Bennington.'

He nodded, and there was that glimpse of pain again. 'I've

already asked around, Ms Blake; everyone said that if anyone can raise my Ilsa so she looks like herself and doesn't know she's dead, you are the only one to go to, and you've turned me down.' He bit his lip again, that swell of muscle showing his control beginning to slip.

Micah said, 'I am sorry for your loss, Mr Bennington, but Anita is the expert on the undead; if she says it would go badly, I'd trust her.'

Bennington's gaze went straight to anger. He turned and put that gaze on Micah. 'It's a terrible thing to lose the one you love, Mr Callahan.'

'Yes, it is,' Micah said.

The two men looked at each other, Micah exuding that calm that helped him talk new shapeshifters down when they were about to lose control, and Bennington giving off that tightly wound rage. He turned back to me. 'Is that your final answer: you won't help me bring her back?'

'It's the only answer I have, Mr Bennington. I'm sorry that I can't help you.'

'Won't help, you mean.'

'I said what I meant – I can't.'

He shook his head, over and over; his face was bleak, as if some light had gone out of him. Maybe it was hope; maybe I'd been his last hope and now it was gone. I would have given him back his hope, if I could have, but I honestly couldn't do what he wanted; no one could.

He turned and looked at the three men, slowly, then back to me. 'Do you love them?'

I thought about telling him it was none of his business, but in the face of such pain, I told the truth. 'Yes.'

'All three of them?'

I thought about quibbling, that I *love*-loved Micah and Nathaniel, but loved Jason as a friend. The fact that I had sex with all of them sort of muddied the waters for most people, but the four of us were clear on how we felt about each other, and all of us knew that Jason was my friend first and everything else second. We were secure, so I gave the short answer: 'I do.'

He looked at all of us again, nodded once, and then opened the door. 'I've never been able to love more than one person at a time. It would be easier if I could.'

I didn't know what to say to that, so I didn't bother. I tried to put my sympathy into my face, and let it go at that.

'Their being here with you proves that at least some of the tallest tales about you are true.'

'You keep leaving me not knowing what to say, Mr Bennington.'

'I thought women always knew what to say.'

'I don't.'

'My wife was a very different kind of woman than you, Ms Blake.'

'I hear that a lot,' I said.

'Please, help me get her back.'

'I can't give her back to you, Mr Bennington. No human being could do what you truly want, no matter how psychically gifted they might be.'

'And what do I truly want?'

'You want resurrection of the body and mind and soul. I'm good, Mr Bennington, maybe the best. But no one, not even me, is that good.'

He left then without another word, closing the door carefully behind him. Micah hugged me. 'That was unpleasant.'

I raised my face for a kiss, which he gave, and hugged him back. 'Unpleasant,' I said. 'That's one word for it.'

Nathaniel hugged me from behind, and I was suddenly sandwiched between my two live-in sweeties. Nathaniel kissed the top of my head. 'Come to lunch, and Jason and I will flirt outrageously, and make you smile.'

'As long as I'm left out of the flirting,' Micah said.

'It's okay that you don't flirt in public,' Nathaniel said, 'you do fine at home.'

Jason came to stand beside us. 'If four's a crowd I can take a hint.'

It was Micah who opened his arm and brought Jason into the group hug, which let Nathaniel do the same. We snuggled together for a moment, and Jason put his face against mine. 'I don't know how you deal with clients all day, Anita.'

'I could do without the grieving relatives, that's for sure,' I said.

'One of these days,' Mary said from behind us, 'you have to tell me how you do that.'

We broke from the hug enough for me to look at her. 'Do what?'

She waved her hands at us all. 'Three of the sexiest men I've seen in weeks and they're all here to take you to lunch. If you find one over thirty, throw him my way.' It made me laugh, which is what she meant it to do. Mary had worked here as long as I had, and she'd seen worse displays of grief than Tony Bennington's.

I smiled to let her know it worked, and tried to shake the

depressing feeling that I'd failed Bennington. I had told him the truth, but sometimes the last thing you want when you're grieving is truth.

'I have a couple that are way over thirty, Mary, but I didn't think you were into vampires.'

She made a girlish squeal, which was a sound that should have been outlawed once you hit the other side of fifty, but Mary could still pull it off. I was under thirty and still couldn't do the squeal without feeling like an idiot. It was never a voluntary sound for me.

'See you after lunch, Mary.'

'If I had all three of them with me, I would make it a long lunch.'

I grinned, and then felt the blush start. I always had blushed easily, damn it.

Mary laughed, until Jason walked over to her and kissed her cheek, and then it was her turn to blush. We left the office laughing, with Mary joining us. 'Go on with you, cheeky kid,' she said to Jason, but was still bright-eyed with the attention.

'Cheeky, hmm,' Jason said. I grabbed his arm and pulled him out the door before he could do whatever was behind that gleam in his eyes. I wasn't sure if Mary would thank me later, or be disappointed.

WE GOT TO a booth in a restaurant that was near enough to my work that we'd walked – Micah and I in our suits, and the other two looking like gym bunnies who'd escaped to be among us mere mortals. They had put on summer-weight workout pants over the shorts, which they'd gotten out of Jason's car. Nathaniel had even added a lightweight jacket. He knew that I wasn't always comfy with a lot of attention, even if I wasn't the one attracting it. Micah looked as cute in less clothes as they did, but he, like me, didn't usually flash unless at home. We were shy, but it was a sliding scale. We were shy in comparison to Jason and Nathaniel, but then so were most people. I appreciated them putting on more clothes and told them so. I also asked them, 'If you had more clothes, why did you wear less to pick me up at work?'

'Mary likes it when we flirt with her,' Nathaniel said.

'So if it had been nighttime and Craig was on duty, you'd have put on more clothes?' I asked.

'Yes,' they said.

I let it go at that, because I'd learned to.

Micah and Jason were at either end of the circular booth,

putting Nathaniel and me in the center, but it was easy for any of us who wanted to sit as close as we wanted until the food came, and then we'd need more elbow room. But until then, Micah and I held hands, but that's too passive a word. We played our fingers up and down on each other's. We made small circles on each other's hands. I drew my nails lightly down the back of his hand, which made him close his eyes, lips parting. He returned the favor by drawing his nails down the inside of my wrist, and that made me have to fight off a visible shudder. 'Okay, point taken, I'll back down.' My voice was breathy.

'You guys are so much fun,' Jason said.

'Yes, they are,' Nathaniel said, and some tone in his voice made me look at him, and I was suddenly very aware that I was staring into his face from inches away. Micah and I were still holding hands, but I was left wondering if I'd somehow neglected Nathaniel. I opened my mouth to ask something that blunt, when he said, 'You and Micah always have to touch each other more than just a hug and a kiss. Until you do there's this tension between you; always.'

'Do I apologize for that?' I asked, and my voice was still breathy.

'No,' he said, voice low, 'you're the same way with me.' His hand found my skirt and began to slide down my thigh until his fingers touched hose. He slid his hand over my hose, to the inner thigh. My free hand grabbed his hand, and my other hand flexed in Micah's, who grabbed back, and the pressure of his hand both helped me think and made me think about both of them, in a way that wasn't helpful at all.

My pulse was suddenly in my throat and it wasn't because I was afraid. Mary had said she'd take a long lunch, and that suddenly didn't seem like a bad idea. I frowned, and tried to think a little better than that.

Nathaniel leaned in and whispered against my face, breath so warm, 'Too much?'

I nodded, not trusting my voice.

'I don't think this is going to make her laugh,' Micah said.

I shook my head.

Nathaniel backed up enough so he wasn't breathing his words directly on my skin. 'I'm not jealous of you and Micah, because you still react as if me touching you is new.'

I turned and looked at him, frowning at little. 'Are you insinuating that other people have gotten tired of you touching them?'

'Now you've gone and made her think,' Jason said. 'Thinking will not make her smile.'

I gave him an unfriendly look.

He held his hands up, as if to say, *Don't shoot the messenger*. 'You know I'm right.'

Nathaniel said, 'I'm saying that other people have wanted me for a night, or a few days a week, or a month, but you never seem to grow tired of me.'

I just looked at him. 'They were crazy.'

He smiled, not the sexy smile, but the big, bright, happy smile. The one I hadn't even known he had in him until we'd been together for months. It made him look even younger than twenty-one, and I had the feeling that maybe that smile was what he might have been if he hadn't lost his family and been on the streets before age ten.

Jason leaned around Nathaniel and said, 'I'm remembering why I don't go to lunch with all of you.'

'Why?' I asked.

He gave us all a look.

'I think Jason feels left out,' Micah said.

It was one of those moments that Miss Manners didn't cover. I had sex with Jason, but he was my friend, not my boyfriend. There was a difference. So if your guy friend and sometimes lover feels left out when you're cuddling your boyfriends at lunch, do you owe him a cuddle?

'I'm closer,' Nathaniel said, 'but I think he'd rather have the kiss from you.'

Jason, being Jason, then put his arm around Nathaniel and said, 'It's nothing personal, dude, but she's not a dude.' He did a drawling movie-dude voice to go with the line.

It made us all smile, and I leaned past Nathaniel to give Jason a quick kiss. It was almost as if now that we had the touching out of the way we could talk.

We'd found out on the walk over that the dance class that they were taking was going well, but the routine that they were trying to teach some of the other dancers from Jean-Claude's clubs had hit a snag.

'You said you'd explain the problem you're having teaching the dancers,' I said.

'I can't convince some of the women from the Circus and Danse Macabre that I'm their teacher, not just a cute guy,' Jason said.

'They don't respect you?' Micah asked.

'They hit on me,' he said.

Micah and I exchanged a glance, then both looked back at him. 'And that's a problem for you, how?' I asked.

He grinned. 'Okay, I love to flirt, but not when I'm teaching.

I can't play favorites, and I can't use the class as a dating pool, because that would be playing favorites. I'm trying to get these women to work harder than they're used to, and they're trying to flirt in part to get out of the hard work.'

Nathaniel explained, 'Most of the human women come from a stripper background, and most strip clubs aren't like Guilty Pleasures, Anita. They don't really want you to dance at most clubs, just move a little and take your clothes off. Jason is asking them to dance, really dance.'

'Dancing is hard work,' he said, 'and some of these women have used their beauty to avoid hard work all their lives.'

'You keep saying *women*,' Micah said. 'I thought you were training up some of the male dancers, too.'

'We are, but most of them came from Guilty Pleasures, and Jean-Claude always made us put on a real show there. The other wereanimals aren't arguing about it, either.'

'They know if they don't do what they're told, it will get back to the head of their animal group,' Micah said.

Jason smiled at him. 'Yeah, Caleb is sooo not happy that you made him move from waiter at Guilty Pleasures to dancer, O Leopard King.'

Micah gave a small frown. 'I didn't make him change jobs; I gave him a choice of jobs that would make him more money, because he was complaining he needed more money. I'm his Nimir-Raj; I helped him brainstorm some alternate jobs. He thought stripping was the lesser evil.'

'We got tired of him bitching,' I said.

Jason grinned. 'He does like to bitch, O Leopard Queen.'

I was queen to Micah's king, but I was still technically human and didn't change shapes. Blood tests had proved I carried several different kinds of lycanthropy inside me, but I stayed human. The lycanthropy virus protected its host from all disease, which should have meant that I couldn't catch a second kind once I caught the first, but my body seemed able to collect them. I was one of about forty people worldwide who had managed to be carriers of multistrains but not shapeshift. We'd been the inspiration for the lycanthropy vaccine that had begun to be used worldwide. My bit for medical science. With every new animal, there was the potential that I could call that animal to me like a vampire. I was really trying not to do that again.

I turned to Nathaniel. 'You recognized Bennington's wife, didn't you?'

He nodded, face serious. 'She was a fur-fucker.'

'A what?' I asked.

Jason explained, 'They're like badge bunnies for cops, or groupies for bands. They just want to fuck us because we turn furry once a month.'

Nathaniel said, 'She had money so she got private dances, but she was like most of the fur-fuckers. She seemed to think that we were animals and wouldn't be able to resist our baser urges, as if because we have a beast inside us we can't say no, or don't have the right to say no.'

Jason frowned. 'I used to do it after work, never for money, but just because a woman was hot, and she wanted me. But after a while it was as if they'd fuck the tiger in the zoo if it wouldn't eat them, and they didn't think of me as much different from that.'

I hugged Nathaniel with one arm and put my other arm past to draw Jason into the hug. 'I'm sorry that people are so stupid.'

Micah leaned in at my back, and we did our best to do a group hug in the booth, which didn't quite work, but still got the job done. Nathaniel and Jason were smiling when we pulled back, and that was the goal.

'Did anyone at the club cross the line with the wife?' I asked.

Nathaniel shook his head. 'Jean-Claude's really strict about that, so no. There are a few dancers and bouncers that will do the fur-fuckers, but she wanted one of us to do it in the private dance area right then. That was her fantasy and she wasn't settling for fucking one of us later in a hotel room, or so she informed Graham, after he offered to meet her after work.'

Graham was a werewolf and a bouncer, not a dancer, but he was cute enough.

'A blow to his ego,' I said.

'Not as bad a hit as the fact that you keep refusing him,' Jason said, and he grinned, knowing it was a sore point with me.

I frowned at him, and then got back on point. 'Did she get kicked out?'

Nathaniel nodded. 'Security had to escort her outside, because she wouldn't take no from us, and she just kept trying to up the price as if we were whores.'

I leaned my face in against his, not sure what to say, because when I'd first met him he had been a prostitute. He'd been a high-priced one catering to an elite clientele, but in the end there had been too many clients who wanted him because a wereanimal could take a lot of damage and still survive. It was too much rough trade, even for someone who enjoyed pain the way Nathaniel did.

'A lot of people think that about strippers,' Jason said.

'I know,' Nathaniel said.

'I thought we were supposed to cheer up Anita,' Micah said, 'not be the gloomy ones.'

They both looked up, exchanged a glance, then Jason grinned at me. 'I think we promised to flirt outrageously.'

'You said that, and just assumed I'd go along,' Nathaniel said.

Jason aimed the grin at him. 'Won't you?'

Nathaniel smiled, shrugged, and nodded.

'Then let the flirting begin,' Jason said.

I was a little nervous about what *outrageously* might mean, but I'd take silly and a little embarrassing over them being sad. But as usual the flirting confused me.

When Jason had said he and Nathaniel would flirt outrageously, I thought they'd meant flirting within our little group, but when the waiter came to our booth, the plans changed. The waiter started out very sure of himself: 'I'm sorry that no one's been to your table.' I was sitting beside Nathaniel, so I got a very good look at what happened to the waiter's face when Nathaniel looked up at him. That's all he did, just raise that face, and those eyes, and stare directly at the waiter – who went from reasonably intelligent and competent to stammering. No, I'm not joking. The waiter began to stammer, a lot of *uhs*, and *hmms*, and words not in their right order. Nathaniel, having noticed the reaction, smiled at him, which didn't help at all. The waiter finally, in desperation, said, 'Drinks, drinks, can I bring you drinks?'

'Yes,' I said, we all said, 'drinks would be good.'

He took our drink orders while staring at Nathaniel, which

meant he didn't write anything down, which led me to wonder if we'd actually get what we ordered, but we were all merciful and let him flee the table for somewhere safe from Nathaniel's charm.

Jason turned to me and Micah. 'Can he flirt with the waiter?'

'No,' we said in unison. Micah said, 'Please don't, because we'll either get great service or terrible service, and we need to get Anita back to work.'

Then, of course, it being me, I felt compelled to ask, 'Do you *want* to flirt with the waiter?'

'Before I was with the two of you I would have, but I know it makes you uncomfortable.'

'Which is why I asked for him,' Jason said.

I looked at Micah, and we had a moment of what I thought was understanding, but being the girl I couldn't trust to silent communication. I had to say something. 'Do we take some of the fun out of things for Nathaniel?'

Nathaniel answered, 'No, I would never trade being able to flirt with strangers for living at our house with you guys. When I could flirt with whoever I wanted, I wasn't very happy; now I'm happy.'

I kissed him, gently, since I was wearing bright lipstick. His mouth came away with a faint hint of red. Jason said, 'Waiter is coming this way; if you want to play with him, you can't be hanging all over Nathaniel.'

I didn't argue with Jason, because if anyone knew the rules for teasing people, it was him. By the time the waiter got to us, we were just sitting there. He had our drink orders correct, which meant we might get good service after all.

He took our orders while looking at Nathaniel as if the

rest of us didn't exist. He spoke to us, even wrote down what we said, but he never looked at anyone else. Nathaniel didn't do anything but just looked pleasantly at him. It had taken me a while to figure out that was flirting, too. Just letting another human being know that you 'see' them is perhaps the most important part of flirting. Nathaniel had taught me that not all flirting is about sex. You flirt, in a way, with friends, family, even a job interviewer; you want them to like you, or you want them to know that you are listening, that you care. I'd learned that I wasn't very good at letting anyone know I liked them unless I was trying to date them. Learning to flirt in a more broad sense had made me a more pleasant person all around, but then it would have been hard to be less pleasant.

There was silence around the table, and I realized that everyone was looking at me; finally even the waiter looked. I blinked up at him. 'I'm sorry, what?'

'What do you want to order?' Micah said.

I had no idea. 'I'm sorry, but I don't know what I want.'

The waiter's eyes flicked back to Nathaniel, then at me, as he said, 'I'll give you a few minutes, then check back.'

I smiled at him encouragingly. He smiled, gave me a brilliant smile that lit his face up. I think it was only because I was sitting close enough to Nathaniel so he could flash that smile at both of us, but I smiled back, and I noticed that he was tanned and his hair was almost black, straight and tucked into a short ponytail, with a long wisp of hair escaping to trace the edge of a triangular face. His eyes were dark, and sparkling with his desire to catch Nathaniel's attention. He was cute, and that was the problem with this kind of flirting. I couldn't figure out how to let someone know I 'saw' them without really seeing them. I couldn't pretend to notice someone. I either noticed them, or I didn't. He flashed that brilliant white smile in his tan and left me to my menu.

'I'm glad we didn't bet on this one,' Jason said, 'I'd have lost.'

Nathaniel looked at him. 'You thought he was gay.'

'The way he reacted to you – yes.'

I was studying my menu, trying to remember what I'd wanted. Some kind of salad, I think. Or had it been the pulled pork sandwich? That was always good.

'But he smiled at both of you, so I'm betting bi.'

'Pulled pork sandwich. I'm going back to work, so I don't have to eat light. But the waiter wasn't smiling at me, he'd noticed he had only looked at Nathaniel and I was the only one close enough to let him look at me and still see Nathaniel.'

'You made him see you when you looked up and smiled,' Nathaniel said.

'Not on purpose,' I said.

'We've all started adopting some of Nathaniel's charms,' Micah said.

I looked at him. 'You, too?'

He nodded, smiled, and looked down, as if he were a little embarrassed. 'I've found that a little charm helps a lot in politics, and you want people to like you; no one is better at getting people to like them than these two.' He ended with a wry tone and a look halfway between amused and disgusted, but ended with a smile.

Jason batted blue eyes at him. 'Aw, that's so sweet; you've been taking lessons in *luuvv* from us.'

Micah scowled at him, and I realized it was a look more reminiscent of me. Did all couples begin to pick up mannerisms from each other? I knew I'd picked up things from Jean-Claude, but I was his human servant, which meant that personality and psychic gifts literally mingled, or were contagious. But then I was Micah's Nimir-Ra, leopard queen, and Nathaniel was my animal to call, so maybe it was the metaphysics still. I'd learned that my initial attraction to Micah had been vampire powers – mine, not Jean-Claude's. The powers of Belle Morte's line were lust and love, with the caveat for most of them that you could only control someone to the degree you were willing to be controlled. For me it truly was a double-edged sword, and with Nathaniel and Micah I'd been willing to be cut to the heart. By the time I'd made Jason my wolf to call, I'd had more control so we were still just friends. Though I'd bound him to me during a crisis, by accident, just reaching out for the metaphysical help that was closest, I hadn't made us fall In Love with each other. I was relieved and I think so was he.

'Do you really not understand that he was flirting with both of us?' Nathaniel asked.

I gave him a look. 'He could smile in your direction looking at me, without staring at you. I think he'd noticed he was only staring at you and it finally embarrassed him.'

Nathaniel looked across me to Micah. 'You saw it. What do you think?'

He took my hand and kissed it, gently. 'I think she doesn't see herself the way we do.'

I tried to pull my hand back. 'I see myself first thing in the morning, and trust me, I don't roll out of bed looking that good.'

He held my hand tighter. 'Haven't we proved by now that we find you fabulous in the morning?'

I scowled at him, but stopped pulling on my hand. 'I was told all my childhood that I wasn't pretty, and you guys love me because of vampire powers. You may not be able to help it.'

Nathaniel's arms encircled me from behind, as Micah came in from the front for a kiss. 'You are beautiful, Anita, I swear it's true,' he whispered. I was tense in their arms, almost panicked; why? My father's second wife had been blond and blue-eyed, tall and Nordic, as had her daughter from her first marriage, and the son they had together later. I loved my brother Josh, but I'd always looked like the dark secret in the family pictures, and Judith had been very quick to explain to friends that I wasn't hers; that my mother had been Hispanic. I'd always blamed my lack of self-esteem on that, but now I realized that wasn't all of it. It wasn't like a buried memory, just one I hadn't looked at before.

'My Grandmother Blake took care of me while my father worked for about a year. I'd just lost my mom, and she told me that I was ugly, that I better not count on finding a husband, but get an education and a job and take care of myself.'

'What?' Micah said. Nathaniel's arms tightened around me.

'Don't make me say it again; it's such a shitty thing to do to a little kid.'

'You know it's not true,' Micah said, studying my face.

I nodded, and then shook my head. 'I guess, not really. I mean, I see how people react to me so I know I clean up well, but I can't really see why you guys react to me. I just see what my grandmother and then my stepmother told me wasn't tall

enough, white enough, pretty enough.' The tightness in my
chest eased the panic flowing away on the realization that even
if I'd been an ugly little girl, a grandmother who loved you
wouldn't have said it. She might have encouraged you to study
hard and get a career, but she wouldn't have told you it was
because you were ugly and no man would have you.

Nathaniel kissed the side of my face as Micah kissed my
lips. I stayed motionless in their arms, letting the knowledge
of that childhood memory wash over me. 'Why did I remember
that now?' I asked, softly.

'You were ready to remember,' Nathaniel whispered. 'We
bring up the pain in pieces so we can look at it in small bites.'

Jason spoke softly from just behind Nathaniel. 'First, you
are beautiful and desirable, and that was evil of her. Second,
one thing I've learned in therapy is that when you feel your
most safe, most happy, is when the really painful stuff rears
its head.'

'I remember Nathaniel's therapist saying that when you
started having bad dreams. Why does it have to work that
way?' I asked, still held between the other two men.

'You feel safe enough and you believe you have enough of
a support network to look at the really bad stuff, so when
your life is going its best, we all have a tendency to dredge
up the worst of our pain.'

I turned in their arms so I could see Jason's face. 'That
sucks,' I said.

He smiled, eyes gentle. 'Big-time suck, yes.' He studied my
face. 'You aren't going to cry, are you?'

I thought about it, figuring out how I felt. 'No.'

'It's okay to cry,' he said.

I shook my head. 'I don't want to cry.'

'You never want to cry,' Nathaniel said.

I couldn't argue that, so instead I let myself soften in their arms, and kissed first Micah, and then turned so I could lay my cheek against Nathaniel's face and whisper, 'I'll cry later, at home.'

'You'll cry when it finally hits you,' he said.

'I don't feel like crying now.'

'How do you feel?' he asked.

'You could read my feelings.'

'You've taught me better psychic manners than that,' he said.

'I came with better manners than that,' Micah said.

I nodded, and then started to sit back on the bench. They moved back to let me. 'I feel sort of hollow, like there's this empty space inside me that I didn't know was there. Fragile – which I hate.'

Jason reached past Nathaniel to pat my thigh, just a friendly touch. 'It's okay, we're here.'

I nodded. That was the problem with loving people: it made you weak. It made you need them. It made the thought of not having them the worst thing in the world. I heard Bennington's words in my head: *It's a terrible thing to lose someone you love.* I knew it for truth, because I'd lost my mother to death when I was eight, and my fiancé in college to his mother's pressure. Come to think of it, that had been because I wasn't blond and Caucasian enough for his family. They hadn't wanted their family tree darkened quite that much. Was it any wonder I had a complex about it? It would have been a miracle if I hadn't.

For a long time after that first love, I'd protected my heart from all takers; now here I sat in a restaurant with two men I loved, and a third who was one of my best friends. How had I been willing to let so many people get so damn close?

The waiter was back at the table. He smiled that brilliant smile at me, and I could see that he was looking at me, not Nathaniel. I started to do what I'd done for years when men reacted to me – scowl and give him The Look – and then I realized that I didn't want to be angry. I smiled at him, let him see that I saw him; I understood he was wasting smiles on me, and I appreciated it. I let myself smile up at him and let the pure happiness fill my face all the way up. The smile wasn't entirely for the waiter; it was for the men around me, yet it made the waiter smile even wider, his eyes shining with it. It wasn't a bad thing to share; in fact, it was a pretty nice thing to share, even with someone you didn't know at all.

Ms Natalie Zell sat across from me with her red hair in an artful tangle of swept waves that managed to be short enough not to go past her shoulders but also gave the impression that she had long hair. It was a good illusion, and probably an expensive one, but from the crème of her designer dress to the nearly perfect skin under its even more perfect makeup – all so understated that, at a glance, you might have been fooled into thinking she wasn't wearing makeup – everything about her breathed money. I'd had enough rich clients to know the taste of someone who had always had money. Two days later I was betting that Natalie Zell was someone who had never wanted for anything and didn't see any reason for that to change. She crooked her pale lips and they caught the light, shining, very sparkly in a subdued sort of way. Old money is seldom gaudy; they leave that for the nouveaux riches.

'I want you to raise my husband from the dead, Ms Blake,' she said, smiling.

I searched her face for signs of grief, but her grayish-green eyes were wide and unmarred with anything but a faint humor and a force of personality quietly controlled. I must have looked into her eyes too long, or too directly, because she lowered her lashes so that I lost eye contact.

'Why do you want Mr Zell raised from the dead?' I asked.

'Does it really matter at the rates your business manager charges for your services?'

I nodded. 'It matters.'

She crossed her long, slender legs under the pale dress. I think she actually flashed me some thigh, but it might have just been habit, and nothing personal. 'My therapist thinks that a last goodbye would help me find closure.'

That was one of the standard reasons that I raised the dead. 'I'll need the name of your therapist.'

Her eyes lost that mild amusement and I caught a flash of that personality that I could feel behind all the pale control. I didn't believe her about the therapist.

'Why do you need his name?' she asked, as she leaned back in the client chair, all elegant nonchalance.

'It's standard to check.' I smiled, and I could feel that it didn't quite make it to my eyes. I could have made the effort, but I didn't. I didn't want her comfortable. I wanted the truth.

She gave me a name.

I nodded. 'He'll have to sign a waiver that he really thinks it's a good idea for you to see your husband raised as a zombie. We've had a few clients who didn't react well to it.'

'I understand that people could be traumatized by a normal animated zombie, all rotted and awful.' She made a face, then leaned a little toward me. 'But you raise zombies that look like real people. My therapist says that Chase will look like he's alive, that he'll even believe he's alive at first. If that's true then how will it be traumatic?'

I was betting that if I called the therapist he'd back her story. Maybe it was her therapist's confidence, but something felt wrong about her reactions. You usually saw grief even through a brave face. Either she was a sociopath or she didn't give a damn about Chase Zell, her late husband.

'So, I raise your late husband as a zombie that can talk and think, and you talk to him and say goodbye, is that it?'

She smiled happily and leaned back in her chair again. 'Exactly.'

'I think you should ask one of the other animators at Animators Inc.'

'But you're the only one that everyone says can raise a zombie that thinks and looks and acts alive.'

I shrugged. 'There are one or two others in this country who can do it.'

She shook her head, the expensive haircut bobbing as she moved. 'No, I've checked. You are the only one that everyone agrees can guarantee that a zombie will be completely lifelike.'

I had a bad thought. 'What do you want your late husband to be able to do one last time, Ms Zell?'

'I want him to be alive one more time.'

'Sex with a zombie, no matter how lifelike, is still considered a crime. I can't help you do that, not legally.'

She actually blushed under the nice makeup. 'I have no intention of doing that with him ever again, and especially not as a zombie. That's . . . that's just . . . disgusting.'

'Glad we agree on that.'

She recovered, though I had shocked her; nice to know I could. 'Then you will raise Chase from the dead for me?'

'Maybe.'

'Why won't you just do this? If it's the money, I'll double your fee.'

I raised an eyebrow. 'That's a lot of money.'

'I have a lot of money. What I need is my husband back among the living for a few more minutes.'

I couldn't tell you what it was that went through her eyes just then, or why I didn't like it. I'd spent too much time around bad people not to look for it in most faces, and I had my share of clients whose lies had created some really awful nights. I'd even had one client who had me raise a husband that she had killed, and he had done what all murdered zombies do – killed his murderer. Until he throttled the life out of her I couldn't command him to do a damn thing. Things like that had made me suspicious of the stories that the nice people across my desk told me.

'What will you do with him for those minutes, Ms Zell?' I asked.

She crossed her arms over her thin chest and scowled at me. She wasn't trying to be pretty anymore, or soft. Her eyes were suddenly more gray than green, and it was a steely gray like a polished gun barrel. 'You know, who the fuck talked to you?'

I shrugged and gave a little smile, letting her pick a name.

'It was that bastard gardener, wasn't it? I should have tried to sharpen the axe myself.'

I kept the vague smile on my face and gave her an encouraging look. It was amazing what people would tell me if I just kept quiet and seemed to know more than I did.

'I'll pay your regular fee, plus a million dollars tax-free so that no one knows but you and me.'

I raised both eyebrows at that. 'That is *a lot* of money.'

'It's not about the money; what I want is revenge.'

I fought my face not to look surprised. I needed her to believe I already knew most of it to keep her talking. 'You can't take revenge on the true dead, Ms Zell. They're dead. It doesn't get much more revengey than that.'

She leaned forward again, hands out, almost pleading. 'But you can make him alive again for me. He'll believe he's alive, right?'

I nodded.

'You can do that without a human sacrifice, right?'

'Most animators can't do it with one,' I said.

She gave me a look. 'Are you that arrogant, or that good?'

'That wasn't arrogance, Ms Zell, just the truth.'

She looked strangely satisfied. 'Then raise him for me. Raise him and let him be alive. He will feel emotions, right?'

'Yes,' I said.

'Fear? Can a zombie feel fear?'

'One that thinks it's alive and looks alive will be afraid. Most of them are afraid when they realize they're in a graveyard. Some of them freak when they see their own tombstone. It's actually best if you don't let them see that. It can make them begin to lose focus on your questions or your vengeance.'

'But he'll see me, know me, and when I hurt him, he'll be afraid of me, right?'

I nodded. 'Right . . .'

'That's perfect. So, you'll do it?'

'Are you honestly going to use an axe on your deceased husband?'

She nodded, and her face was very firm and sure of itself. Her eyes glinted and the gray seemed to get even darker, like clouds before it storms. 'Oh, yes, I am. I'm going to chop the bastard up while he begs me to stop. I want him to think I'm killing him for real.'

I studied her face and wanted to ask if she was joking, but I knew the answer. 'You want the last memory you will ever have of your husband to be you chopping him up?'

She nodded.

'How long were you married?'

'Almost twenty-five years,' she said, which made me put her on the almost-fifty side of forty, though she didn't look it.

'A man who you married, lived with, slept with, loved at some point, for twenty-five years, and you want to play axe murderer all over his ass?'

'More than anything in the world,' she said.

'What did he do to piss you off this much?'

'That's none of your business,' she said, and her face said she believed I'd accept that answer. Apparently now that we'd agreed on a price she thought she could be arrogant.

'It is if you want me to raise him. Some crimes, some magicks, some problems in life can affect a zombie, make it harder to control. What did he do that was so terrible?'

'He told me he never wanted children. That they would interfere with his business and our social circle, and because I loved him I abided by his rules. Other friends would skip a few pills and come up accidentally pregnant, but I played fair. Chase didn't want children so we didn't have them.' Her eyes were distant as if seeing something other than my office, something sad and faraway.

'If you wanted children then I'm sorry that he cost you that chance.'

She focused on me again, and now the rage was in her eyes, her face. God, she was angry. 'Two weeks ago a young man came to my door. He told me his mother had recently died and that he found letters. He showed me letters from my husband to his mother. There were pictures of them on vacations together. He took her to Rome, but wouldn't take me. He took her to Paris, but wouldn't take me. He once told me that I was one of the least romantic women he'd ever met; it was one of the reasons that he wanted me to be his wife and partner, because he knew that I wouldn't let sentiment get in the way of getting wealthy and successful, because I wanted it as badly as he did.'

'You've always been wealthy?' I asked.

She nodded. 'It was my money that he used to start his company, but he made even more. There was a letter to this woman where he literally said that if he hadn't signed a prenuptial agreement where he'd have to give up controlling interest in his company and have no money that he would have divorced me and stayed with her and their son.'

The look on her face was bleak, like someone who had seen the worst possible thing and lived. She knotted those slender, perfectly manicured hands in her lap and continued to stare past me at things I couldn't see.

'That must have been very painful to read,' I said.

She didn't react.

'Ms Zell,' I said softly.

She shook herself, like a bird settling its feathers, and gave me a hard look. I'd seen a lot of hard looks in my day, but this was a good one. I believed she meant to do exactly what she'd said with her shiny new axe.

'How soon can we schedule it?' she asked.

'We can't,' I said.

'What do you mean?'

'I won't do it,' I said.

'Don't be silly, of course you will.'

'No, Ms Zell, I won't.'

'Two million beyond your fee. Two million dollars that no one knows about but us.' She seemed very sure of herself.

I shook my head. 'It's not about money, Ms Zell.'

'You have to do this for me, Ms Blake. You're the only one who can raise a zombie that can feel real fear and real pain.'

'I couldn't guarantee that he'd feel the same pain he would have felt when he was alive,' I said. I tried to concentrate on the details so I wouldn't concentrate on other things.

'But he will feel pain, real pain?'

'He'll be able to feel. I've had zombies stumble on rocks and fall. They react like it hurts.'

'Perfect,' she said, and that one word was full of so much anticipation.

It made my stomach clench to realize what she was anticipating. 'Let me test my understanding, Ms Zell, just so we're clear. You want me to raise your husband, Chase, from the dead so that he will think he's alive and be able to feel terror and pain while you chop him up with an axe. Do you realize that an axe won't kill a zombie, so he'll keep thinking and being afraid even if you chop him to bits? He'll be afraid until I lay him to rest again.'

'I don't want you to lay him to rest. I want his pieces buried as they are, so that he'll be buried alive and aware until he rots away.'

I did the long blink at her, the one I reserve for moments when I can't think of a damned thing to say. I finally found something to say: 'No.'

'What?' she asked.

'No, as in no, I won't do it.'

'Three million,' she said.

'No,' I said.

'How much will it take?' she asked.

'You don't have that kind of money.'

'Yes,' she said, 'I do.'

'Jesus, woman, if you are sane enough to understand what you are asking me to do, then it is maybe the worst thing I've ever heard of one human being doing to another. That should frighten you, Ms Zell. It really should if you knew the kind of crimes I've worked.'

'You do a lot of serial killers and rogue monsters. I did my research on you, Anita Blake.'

'Good for you, but you are a nasty piece of work.'

'I don't care what you think of me as long as you do what I want.'

I pushed back from my desk. 'No.' I stood up.

She finally realized I was serious, and she looked afraid. Of all the emotions she could have felt I hadn't expected fear. 'If not money, then what? What do you want, Anita? Name it and if money can buy it, it's yours. What do you want?'

'From you, absolutely nothing.'

'If not for you, then your boyfriends. I had you researched

and surely someone in your life must need things that money can buy.'

'Get out,' I said.

'I won't take no for an answer. You're the only animator who can give me Chase alive enough for him to suffer. I want him to suffer, Anita.'

'Yeah, I heard that part.' I started around my desk. I was going to open the door and get her the fuck out of my office. She stood up, and in her heels she was almost a foot taller than me. She moved between me and the door. I could have manhandled her, but the business manager, Bert, frowned on us bruising people while on office property.

'I heard that some of your vampire kills aren't exactly on the books all legal and nice. Everyone knows you've murdered people, Anita.' She was actually right, but they had all been people trying to kill me, or people who had threatened me, or monsters who were trying to kill me, then eat me, or who were threatening to hurt people I was trying to protect. I didn't lose sleep over any of my kills.

'First, it's Ms Blake to you. Second, people say a lot of shit about me. I wouldn't believe it all.' Once upon a time I'd been a bad liar, but that had been a long time ago.

'I'll take proof to the police about some of your crimes. You'll lose that badge of yours, if not more.'

'And I'll tell the police what you wanted me to do, because anyone who would really do what you're describing would do something to a live person.' I studied her face. 'How's his illegitimate son's health lately?'

Her face flickered uncertainly.

'If anything happens to him I will make sure the police come to your door.'

'You don't know his name.'

'Oh, please, like I couldn't find that out. He's probably got a page on the Internet somewhere where he's talked all about his father being Chase Zell.'

She frowned at me, as though she was wondering if I was right.

'Nothing happens to the kid, or you will not have enough money to keep yourself out of jail, or at least the nut house.'

'I am not crazy, Ms Blake. I'm a woman scorned.'

'He was married to you for twenty-five years. I think the poor bastard suffered enough.'

That was it. She turned on the stiletto points of her expensive shoes and stalked out. If I'd known that that would make her leave I'd have said it sooner. Seemed this was my week for people wanting my very 'alive' zombies for very bad purposes.

TWO WEEKS PASSED before I went back to the restaurant where Micah, Nathaniel, and Jason had flirted with the waiter and, all right, so had I. This time I was at a table not a booth, and all by my lonesome. Though honestly I'd eaten more lunches alone in my adult life than with anyone else. The workers at Animators Inc. had staggered schedules so no one had lunch at the same time. Sometimes I brought a book; sometimes it was just good to get out of the office. Today I had actually brought the latest copy of *The Animator*, our trade publication. There were a couple of articles I'd been wanting to read, so I'd order food, read, and hopefully learn something.

My waitress was petite, blond, and female when I ordered drinks, but when the drinks came my waiter was tall, black-haired, and male. It was the waiter from the time before. He put down my Coke, smiled, and said, 'I traded tables with Cathy; I hope you don't mind.'

I shook my head, smiled back. 'I don't mind.'

His gave me that even brighter smile that I remembered from last time. I did what I'd learned last time; I smiled back. It would take two more trips back and forth from the table for me to realize that he thought I was flirting with intent. It was when he stayed at my table talking after my food had arrived that I realized I'd made some kind of tactical error. It was one thing to flirt in the safety of my group, with Nathaniel and Jason to take some of the heat and Micah to look on, but a totally different experience with just me and the waiter. Crap.

His name was Ahsan. He was a college student. He was a theatre major with a minor in literature. He was graduating this year and going on to start his master's program. His goal was to teach at a college, unless his own acting career took off. I learned all this because I couldn't figure out how to stop the conversation. I had flirted first, so it was my fault, and if something is my fault, I try to fix it. But Ahsan was like that scene in *Fantasia* with Mickey Mouse and the brooms carrying water buckets. I'd flirted and gotten the game started, but I had no idea how to stop it. I mean, I could have been blunt – my usual – but I had started it, and so was there a way to gracefully retreat? By now I was pretty certain that he thought I'd come back by myself so I could flirt more freely with him. Eek. I was remembering why I didn't flirt for fun – because I didn't know how. I could flirt with intent of dating or sex, but I sucked at casual flirting. Shit.

I would have tried to play the age difference card, but he was Nathaniel's age exactly, so I couldn't claim that an eight-year age difference weirded me out. I was debating on exactly what I could do to let him down gently, or whether I was irritated enough to let him down hard, when I felt energy. Not just regular human psychic energy, but shapeshifter energy. It was someone powerful enough that it raised the hair on my arms and crawled down my back, to see if it could find my own beasts. Those shadows inside me moved almost like a hand caressing deep within my body. God, he was powerful. Either he was a bad guy letting me know he was here, or he'd picked up my own beasts and thought I was a real shapeshifter. Some of their societies encouraged them to mark territory. One of the ways to do that without a fight was simply let the power out. It was a safe way of saying, *Don't fuck with me*. Or, it was a bad guy, and a threat. I wouldn't know until too late, so I treated it as bad guy: better paranoid than dead.

I smiled sweetly up at Ahsan and said, 'I'm sorry, Ahsan, it's been great talking to you, but I've got to get back to work. I need the check.'

'Can I have your number?'

'How about you give me your number, when you give me the check?'

He wasted more smiles on me, but hurried back through the busy restaurant to get the check and scribble his number on something. But at least the nice waiter wouldn't be standing at my table when the bad guy walked up. There was the remote possibility that it was a sort of preliminary flirting attempt. Some of the really powerful lycanthropes were always searching for a mate to match their power. It helped you control your animal group and keep other shapeshifters from trying to mess with you. But this felt like too much for flirting. The only reason to do the power that was making the air thick and hot and hard to breathe was to mark his metaphysical territory and tell me that he was bigger and badder than I was. Fine with me. I took my gun out from under my arm, as discreetly as I could, and put my hand under the table, gun and all.

I didn't try to draw my own version of shapeshifter power. One, I wasn't as powerful as what was coming toward me. I knew that just from that roil of power. Two, sometimes when I drew my power out it got out of hand; just because I didn't change shape didn't mean the beasts inside me didn't want out. They did. They'd damn near torn me apart from inside before I got a handle on the control. But it wasn't just the pain; there was always the chance that one day I'd shift for real, and a crowded restaurant wasn't the place for it. Also, if it was some misguided macho flirting attempt, then I would let him know he'd misread what I was, and maybe he'd go away.

There was so much power that I couldn't tell what direction he was moving in from. It was like being in the middle of some kind of heat storm. Fuck this; I had a power colder than this, and I'd used it before to keep my own beasts from rising, because lycanthropy is a thing of life, so hot-blooded it's almost more alive than the rest of us. I drew my necromancy, which was always with me. It was like opening a fist that I always had to keep so tightly closed. It was a colder power, closer to vampire than wereanimal. It swept outward through the tables; a few sensitives shivered, but it wouldn't hurt them. It wouldn't do anything to them, because nothing dead walked during the day aboveground, at least not in this town. I used my power like cold water on the heat of his power, because sex I knew; he tasted male. It worked even better than I'd hoped, like water on fire, so that the 'blaze' he'd thrown out around him like a distraction went out, and only the core burn was still bright. I saw him walking through the tables toward me, and his body was edged with a wavering shine of power like some kind of ghostly heat. It was an interesting effect, as if my necromancy pushed his power back. I hadn't visualized it working quite like that, but I filed it away as useful.

I looked at him, and he looked back. We looked at each other across the few yards of space. The moment our eyes met, I knew this wasn't about romance, even shapeshifter romance. He was tall, a shade over six feet, unless he was wearing boots with heels, then he was just under. His hair was pale and shaved close to his head. It was oddly military, but he didn't seem like a soldier, or not one that the government trained. He stood there in his black suit jacket, black button-up shirt, and black jeans. Even his belt buckle was black, probably because silver things attract bullets in a firefight. He started walking toward me again, his big hands out to his sides showing him unarmed, but I wasn't fooled; the suit jacket didn't fit quite right on his left hip, which made him right-handed, and the gun big enough to ruin the line of the jacket.

He moved carefully toward my table, hands still out at his sides, palms forward so I could see he held nothing. But I knew better; he was a shapeshifter, which meant that bare-handed he was stronger, faster, and more deadly than any human in here. They didn't need claws and teeth to break your neck, just speed and strength, and that he would have.

'That's close enough,' I said, before he got quite to the table; if I could have figured out a way to keep him farther back without yelling and drawing attention to us, I would have done it.

He stopped obediently, but his power slapped out at mine, and my nostrils flared with the scent of him. He'd had to call more of his beast to chase back my colder power. I smelled the thick, heavy, heat-washed scent of lion. The lion inside me raised her head and looked up at me, if something that lived inside your body could look up at you. It was the way my mind visualized it so I could 'see' the beasts and not lose what was left of my sanity.

'Good kitty,' I said, and I wasn't talking to the pale gold image in my head. That image sniffed the air and gave a low ·purr. She liked what she smelled, which meant he was as powerful as I feared. The lions, especially the lions, demand a partner that's strong. It probably had something to do with the fact that real lion males will kill all the cubs when they take over a new pride; when your babies are at stake, you want a male that can defend them.

The man's thin lips gave an even thinner smile, but he nodded, as if somehow knowing he was a cat had won me a point. He sniffed the air and gave me a more serious look. He smelled my lioness, and it seemed to surprise him. He hadn't known that I held lion inside me: good. It meant he didn't know everything about me: even better.

His eyes actually slid to the side, and I fought not to look where he was looking. I gave only the edge of my vision in that direction. He was too close to me for me to risk taking my gaze off of him completely. He probably wasn't going to jump me here, but I wasn't sure, so I only saw Ahsan working his way toward me out of the corner of my eye. The shapeshifter turned and watched him completely, not looking at me at all. Was it an insult, or a show of trust?

Ahsan paused before he got to the table, shivering a little. He felt some of the psychic energy wafting around us. He got a point for that. Psychic nulls don't survive well around me. I didn't want to date him, but I didn't want to get him killed, either. He glanced at the man still standing near my table, but not 'at' my table. It was suddenly not just a dangerous situation, but socially awkward. Perfect.

Ahsan looked from one to the other of us, his smile faltering. 'Is this another . . . friend?' He hesitated way too long before settling on that last word.

'He's not a friend,' I said.

'Coworker,' the shapeshifter said, voice absolutely ordinary, even pleasant. 'I just saw Anita getting ready to leave and thought I might get her table. There isn't another empty one.'

Ahsan relaxed. I didn't, because the stranger had managed to calm the waiter and subtly threaten everyone in the restaurant. I fought to let my breath out slow and even, and kept the gun aimed on the main body mass of the stranger. Though with his height, and the table height, he'd better hope I didn't have to pull the trigger, because the main mass I would hit was low, as in below the waist. To hit higher I'd have to be willing to show the gun to the restaurant, and I was hoping not to have to do that. He was right; the restaurant was packed full of innocent bystanders. Packed full of human bodies that the silver-plated bullets would kill just as surely as the shapeshifter; fuck. Not to mention that the amount of power he'd displayed meant he could probably put out just claws on his human hands without having to shift completely, which would have given me time to shoot him. But claws are like switchblades – fast. He could slice up the humans faster than I could kill him. The situation was just chock-full of bad choices.

The lioness inside me began to pace slowly upward, as if

she really could. I knew it was a comforting illusion my mind created, but she walked up a path, and that meant she was coming closer to the surface of me. I did not need to try to shift in the restaurant. It would make me unable to concentrate on the bad guy. I worked at calming my pulse, slowing my breathing. I could control this.

Ahsan wasted another brilliant smile on me, and I fought to smile back as he handed me the faux-leather holder that contained the check. I had one of those moments that no one ever seems to have in movies. How did I pay the check with one hand while keeping the gun aimed in the right direction with the other hand, and actually keep my attention on someone only a few feet away who could probably move in a blur so fast it couldn't be followed with the human eye?

I opened the holder with my left hand, keeping my right and the gun under the table. If I hadn't thought it would make Ahsan call the cops, or talk to a manager who would call the cops, I might have flashed the gun to see if that cooled the flirting, but I wasn't ready to escalate – yet. There was an extra piece of paper folded in with the check. Normally, I'd have unfolded it and looked, but I was trying to keep my attention on the shapeshifter. I took the paper and asked Ahsan, 'Your number?'

He nodded, and smiled more happily.

I knew my smile wasn't up to his, and I thought, What would Nathaniel do? I did my best to put that look into my eyes, but the smile that went with it was not Nathaniel's, it was all mine, a little bit of come-hither and a little bit of threat, as if to say, *When you take a bite I might bite back*. It had been Jason who first explained my smile to me, but it was an honest smile, my life being the way it is. It didn't dissuade Ahsan one little bit. His smile went from bright to serious, and his eyes got that look that a man gets sometimes when he sees something he really likes. Great, now I'd been too intriguing. I should not have to flirt with someone while I'm trying to threaten someone else with a gun; it was too hard to do both.

I glanced at the shapeshifter, and he was smiling wider, as if he understood my discomfort, or maybe I just amused him. But there was wariness in his eyes that hadn't been there before. I wasn't sure what it meant, but I'd done something that made him more nervous. If I could only figure out what, maybe I could do it again. Once I'd been able to use my petite, female packaging to fool the bad guys, but my reputation among the preternatural set had forced most bad guys to ignore the package and treat me like what I was: a predator that specialized in other predators.

I did the only thing I could think of: I slipped Ahsan's number into my jacket pocket, and fished out the credit card I'd tucked in the same pocket. I put it in the little faux-leather holder and handed it back to him. I smiled one more time, turned back to my 'coworker,' and said, 'I didn't think you worked today.'

Ahsan took the hint and left us alone.

He started walking slowly closer, hands still out. I didn't tell him to stop, because I realized that the only way to make certain where my bullets landed was to have him so close I couldn't miss. I was gambling that my own faux-shapeshifter speed would let me shoot him before he killed me. Maybe he wasn't here to kill me, but whatever he was here for it was nothing good. I would have bet serious money on that.

He got to the edge of the table, hands spread a little more, and said, 'May I sit down, because I'd rather not have you shoot me where you're pointing right now.' He smiled happily as he said it, but the smile never touched his eyes. I knew that smile, those cold eyes. I'd worked with too many men who had it, and seen it in the mirror too often.

'Sure,' I said, 'sit there.' I nodded toward the chair that would put him beside me, rather than across.

He started to tuck the chair closer to the table, and I said, 'No, keep far enough away from the table so I can see that your gun stays in its holster.'

He gave a little nod, and angled his chair more toward me, one ankle on his knee, so that it was that very guy stance that some did, as if they wanted to frame their groin for inspection. I wasn't interested, but the lioness was, because she was one of the few beasts inside me that didn't have an equivalent on the outside. It meant she was way more interested in other lions than was comfortable for me. There was one werelion who was applying pretty hard for the job, but I kept avoiding him. I had enough men in my life.

I had slowed the lioness with my breathing and my pulse, but the image that she put in my head was not very human. She wanted me to drop to my knees and rub across him. She wanted more of his scent on us, more of his skin on us. With a gun in my hand, it was easier to push the thoughts down. I let her know that we were in danger, and that did seem to calm all my beasts. They understood danger, and through me, they knew what a gun could do.

The man kept his hands on his knees, and I moved so that the gun was angled more solidly at his chest. There'd be no collateral damage at this distance, because fast as he might be, he wasn't faster than a speeding bullet from less than three feet.

'Just so we're clear,' I said, 'if you try to move fast, I will simply pull the trigger, because I know once you move for real it's my only hope at this range.'

He nodded, still smiling, so that from a distance it would look like we were being friendly. 'You moved me in close so you wouldn't accidentally hit the nice humans. I smell you, Anita; I know I'm not the only kitty-cat at the table. It's a weakness to care too much about your pets.'

I frowned. 'Do you mean humans?'

He nodded, still smiling.

'I carry a badge; it's sort of my job to care about them.'

'First, let's be very clear. If anything happens to me, then your people die.'

'What people? You mean the people in the restaurant?'

'No, but knowing you care does make it easier.' He nodded a little behind me. 'It's a visual.'

'If I even feel you move too much, I will just pull this trigger.' The lioness in me snarled at the air, and the edge of it trickled out between my lips. It made the threat better, but it was not a good sign for my control. *One problem at a time, Anita, one problem at a time.* Talking to myself wasn't a good sign, either, but sometimes using my own name reminded me that I wasn't the beast, but the person.

'I believe you,' he said, voice dropping lower. 'I will sit very, very still, kitten.'

I would have protested the nickname, but I had called him kitty first. I turned and found Ahsan almost at our table. He smiled, thinking I was looking for him, and in a way I was, because there was a second bad guy behind him. He had a blond skater's cut, complete with a wedge of bangs that covered his right eye completely. He wore an oversized tank top and baggy shorts, which could hide a lot of weapons. How did I know he was a bad guy? Maybe it was the gun in his hand that he hid under the oversized shirt. The shirt was so big it hung off one shoulder and showed off that his upper body hit the gym a lot.

If I'd had concentration left for it, I'd have tried to taste whether he was shapeshifter or human. If he was shifter he was trying to hide his energy, or the energy coming off his friend drowned him out. Either way, he was following behind Ahsan, and he had his gun out. He was wearing exercise gloves like for biking or weight lifting, the ones that covered all the front of the hand. Leather gloves in this heat – seriously paranoid, or seriously had his prints in the crime-stopper databases. Either way, I got to watch him follow the waiter to 'our' table. The threat was no longer subtle.

'Nick,' the man at the table called out, in a happy voice, 'thought I'd have to eat lunch alone.'

The second man grinned at us both, and it reminded me of Jason's grin. It even filled his blue eyes with laughter. He was damn near six feet and not built like Jason at all, but there was something about him that reminded me; maybe it was a meaner edge of that urge Jason always had to fight off, to keep pushing a situation. That was not a good personality trait in someone with a gun.

Ahsan made room for Nick to take the seat nearest the waiter, so that he and the first guy were sitting across from each other, and so Nick's gun was still very close to Ahsan. I still hadn't figured out how to sign the check one-handed, I couldn't keep the gun pointed at both of them anyway. I'd gone from having some tactical advantage to none. Shit.

Ahsan had pity on me and held the pieces of paper while I signed, and I even managed to give him a generous tip. I mean, if I was going to get him shot it was the least I could do. His fingers brushed my hand, and I realized he thought I'd given him an excuse to touch me. Normally, it would have bugged me, but I had bigger problems than his fingers tracing over my hand. I even let him take my hand and give it a little squeeze. God knows what he might have said, but he glanced at my two 'coworkers' and just wasted one more really good smile on me. I tried to return it, but wasn't sure I managed. His smile didn't fade, though; maybe he assumed that I didn't want to show too much around my 'coworkers'?

'He's cute,' Nick said, in a voice that matched the hair and the clothes, but his hand, under the table, was pointing at me. I didn't have to see the gun to know it was there, and that he'd hit me somewhere between stomach and chest.

'He's okay,' I said.

'Oh, come on, don't play coy. He's hot.'

'Enough, Nick, this is business.'

'Just because it's business doesn't mean it can't be fun.'

'Nick would enjoy killing your waiter, Anita.'

'Yes, I would,' Nick said, and smiled when he said it, all the way up to his baby blues.

'Sociopath much?' I asked, smiling sweetly, my gun still

pointed at the other man, because I wasn't sure what Nick would do if he saw my arm move in his direction.

'All the damn time,' he said, cheerfully.

'What do you want?' I said, trying to keep an eye on both of them for movement and knowing the moment they flanked me I was not going to win. I could take one of them, but not both, not like this. My pulse tried to speed up, and that made the lioness that had been behaving herself so nicely begin to walk up that metaphysical path. If I lost too much control of my body, she'd ride my pulse and breathing as near the surface of me as she could get. The beasts found my inability to shapeshift very frustrating, and that could lead to some very painful moments for me while they tried to claw their way out. I hadn't had any of them do that in a while, but the bad guy *would* have to be a werelion. Worst choice possible; I might have thought the bad guys did that on purpose, but the first one had been genuinely surprised to smell lion on the air. It was just a bad coincidence.

I heard Nick take in a deep breath. I didn't have to see the movement to know he was sniffing the air.

'Don't move toward her,' the first man said; 'we're all going to be very calm, and that way we walk out of here without hurting any of the nice people.'

'She smells like lion,' Nick said, 'but it's different, somehow.'

'Shut the fuck up, Nicky.' The first guy was angry, and that made his power flare again, which made my lion trot faster. I tried to call my necromancy stronger, to calm all this hot-bloodedness, but Nick chose that moment to let me know that he was powerful, too.

Nick's power smashed into me like a blow. It stole my breath, so that the blood in my head was suddenly loud and roaring. The lioness snarled, because it wasn't just me it had hit.

'We're working, Nicky, not dating,' the first man said, and there was an edge of growl to his voice that you might have mistaken for just a low bass voice, but I knew better. My lioness knew better.

My breath came back in a small gasp. 'What the hell was that for?'

'You put your power all over her,' Nicky said, and he sounded sullen. He had enough power to be in the running for top lion, but there were other things to consider besides brute power. Sullen is not my favorite thing.

'You know why I did that,' first man said.

The lioness began to pace more slowly up that hidden path. I felt caution in her, and that wasn't her usual thought process. Something about the second lion's energy had made her think more deeply than normal. I would have loved to ask why, or what, but she was truly animal and they didn't think like that. Something had made her hesitant, almost afraid. But what?

'Yeah, it was part of the plan,' Nicky said, 'supposed to show her how powerful you are so she'd cooperate. Did you feel what she could do with her powers over the dead?' Nicky shivered, and I hoped his finger didn't spasm on the trigger. 'It was like water on fire, but it was power. So much power, Jacob, so much power.' Again, he did that shiver, but this time he did move his arm under the table so the gun was pointed at the floor. I appreciated the caution, and it made me think better of Nicky's wisdom score.

Jacob's power lashed out, not at me, but at his friend. I got the curl of it like a hot wave washing against my legs. It made me startle, and it was my turn to move the gun to the floor. 'I don't mind shooting you, but I'd like it to be on purpose, not because you've made me twitch.'

'Then keep it pointed at the floor,' Nicky said. His power smashed out at his friend, and again I caught that glancing blow. They were both very powerful; it was just a matter of flavor, not strength.

'Stop this, Nick,' Jacob said.

'Do you know how long it's been?' Nick asked.

'Shut up,' Jacob said, and then he turned to me. "We knew about the wolves and the leopards, and we heard you cut quite a swath up in Vegas through the weretigers. You've got Jason Schuyler for your wolf to call, and Nathaniel Graison for your leopard, and even a leopard king in Micah Callahan, and we hear you brought some tigers back from Vegas and have bonded with them. You stole one of Chicago's master vampire's werelions to come down and take over your local pride. He's your Rex, your lion king. You're supposed to be all mated up.'

I didn't like him listing my boyfriends, not one little bit, but he was wrong on one thing. Haven, the local Rex, was not my mate. I had slept with him, but he didn't share well enough. He'd proven that when he slept over one night and started a fight with Micah, Nathaniel, and me the next morning. Haven had been surprised that I'd joined in on the other men's side. He'd said, 'The women don't interfere.' I told him he had the wrong girl, and to get out. He'd actually apologized, which for him was a lot, but he was still not on my favorites list. 'You got a point?' I asked the current problem werelion.

'Your Rex is lying about you and him. Your lioness doesn't belong to him.'

'I don't belong to anyone.'

'Liar, you belong to a lot of people, but you don't belong to Haven. He's put out the word that no more werelions need apply for your bed, because you're his.'

'My dance card is full, so if his lies keep the others away, fine with me.'

'But it isn't fine with your lion,' he said. He shook his head.

'We didn't know you were an unmated werelion. We wouldn't have taken the job if we had.'

'Why not, and what job?' I asked.

'We're being unprofessional, and I apologize for that, but you've caught us off guard.'

'Why are you here, Jacob?' I asked; maybe if I used his name it would speed things along.

'I'm going to reach into my jacket for a cell phone. I have pictures on it to show you. You aren't going to like them. You're going to get angry with us, but remember we were hired to do this, it's nothing personal.' He looked past us. 'Your waiter is coming back.'

'He's probably going to take your orders,' I said.

'Would it really bother you if I killed him?' Nicky asked.

I finally realized that this problem, whatever it really was, wasn't going to be settled by guns at the table. I stopped worrying about keeping an eye on both of them and just looked at Nicky. I gave him the full weight of my unfriendly gaze.

He blinked the one big blue eye I could see. 'Nice look. It really has me quaking in my boots,' he said.

'You haven't seen anything yet,' I said.

'Tease,' he said, low.

Ahsan was back at the table. He wasted smiles on me and I was torn between wanting him away from the table and warning him. 'Can I take drink orders?'

'No,' Jacob said, 'we got called back to work, so no time for lunch. Just give us a few minutes to fill Anita in on the problem, and you'll get your table back.'

He nodded, put his tablet away, and flashed me another brilliant smile. I tried to give one back, but knew my eyes didn't hold it. I couldn't pretend that well. He left us alone, and he would tell the rest of the wait-staff to avoid the table.

'Show me the pictures,' I said.

Jacob spread his suit jacket carefully with two fingers and reached in just as gingerly with his other hand to lift out a cell phone. It was another one with a large screen like Bennington had had for his wife's pictures.

'If you do anything violent, we will hurt some of these nice people,' Jacob said.

'I'll rip the hot waiter's throat open, just for you,' Nicky said, almost a whisper, and smiled while he said it.

'I'm more practical, Anita. I'll hurt whoever is close,' Jacob said.

I nodded. 'The foreplay is getting tiresome, just show me.' But I didn't like the buildup; it promised that whatever they were going to show me would be bad. My pulse was speeding up, but the lioness was not hurrying toward the surface of me. She was afraid; afraid of these men, these lions. She was attracted to male werelions, never afraid. What was wrong with these two that she could sense?

Jacob made the screen light up, pressed something on it,

and said, 'When you want to see the next picture, just slide this with your finger.'

The first picture was of Micah, Nathaniel, and me on the sidewalk holding hands; laughing. The next picture showed Jason leaning in from just behind us, me leaning back listening. We were all smiling. The next picture was a bad angle, and too far away, but it showed us at the booth in this restaurant the day we all came in together. I watched the pictures of that lunch slide across the screen.

'Is there a point to this?' I asked.

'Keep going,' Jacob said.

I went back to the screen and found pictures of Micah driving, going into office buildings, going into the television station for an interview. The next images were of Nathaniel going into Guilty Pleasures at night for work, going down the alley where the dancers' entrance was, then daylight and going in to practice the new dance routine on the stage without customers. Jason was in some of those shots. Jason going into the club at night and driving his new car around town. Jason parking at the Circus of the Damned parking lot, and pictures following him all the way to the door.

I swallowed past the pulse that was trying to come out my throat, and gave a cold, blank face to them. 'So you've been following my boyfriends, what of it?'

'You're almost to the end of the pictures,' he said.

I kept sliding my finger and moving the pictures. I saw Micah walking down the sidewalk, toward an office building. I knew he had meetings all day. But this time there was a picture, then a picture of the camera used to take it; same street, same everything, but a second camera taking an image of the other camera. Then the next image was of a rifle, a very nice sniper rifle. The next image was back on Micah, and the last shot was of the camera and the rifle side by side.

'Is that it?' I asked, and my voice was squeezed down tight.

'The other two are still asleep. They worked last night, but when they get up we'll have men on them, too.'

'You obviously know our schedules. Now what do you want?' I put the phone down and let him slide it across the table to himself.

'First, if we don't check in with our sniper, he shoots Micah when he comes out from the meeting.'

I nodded. 'So I can't shoot you here.'

'No,' he said.

I nodded, small little nods over and over. I wasn't thinking very clearly, but I had enough sense to put my gun back in its holster. It went in smoothly from all that practice, even while the rest of me was frozen. I couldn't think. It was like a great roaring silence in my head, but it wasn't quiet. It was filled with a sound like wind, or storm.

'Good,' Jacob said, 'come with us, quietly, and no one has to get hurt.'

'What do you want me to do?'

'We want you to raise the dead for us.'

'You know you can just make an appointment for that.'

'You've already turned the job down,' he said.

That made me look at him. 'I don't know what you're talking about.'

'Come outside with us, let us pat you down for weapons, and we'll take you to our employer. Then it will all be explained.'

'I would do it before your Nimir-Raj comes out from his meetings,' Nicky said. 'You want us to call our friend the sniper before he comes outside again.'

I stared at him, did the long blink as if I were having trouble focusing. I guess I was; I felt damn near light-headed. I never fainted, but part of my brain was thinking about it. Crap. I had to do better than this, had to be stronger than this.

I nodded again and got up, but I had to touch the table to steady myself.

'You're not going to faint, are you?' Nicky said.

'No,' I said. I took in a lot of air, let it out slow, did it a second time. 'I don't faint.' I started walking, and really wished I were in jogging shoes rather than high heels, but you never plan to be kidnapped, so you're never dressed for it.

I caught my heel on a chair leg, and Nicky grabbed my arm. All touch makes metaphysical powers more. My lioness snarled inside me, her power lashing out, and a slap like claws, saying, *Get back!*

Nicky staggered a little, but didn't let go of my arm. He squeezed hard enough for it to hurt, and growled out, 'That hurt!'

'It was supposed to,' I said.

'Let her go, Nicky.' Jacob was up with us, using his taller body to try to block the view.

Nicky growled at him, still holding my arm.

The lioness and I were in agreement, as we lashed out at them both. The visual was of claws slicing at them. They both reacted as if the pretend claws had weight to them. Jacob touched Nicky's wrist. 'Let her go, now, before we cause a scene.'

'She started it.'

'Bullshit,' I said.

Jacob made the other one let me go. They stepped back, gave me some room. But both their beasts were watching me. It was that feeling that you might get on the grasslands surrounded by all that gold, wavy grass, and you stop because you feel something watching you. I knew I had not just the men's attention, but also that part of them that turned furry once a month was staring holes in me.

I heard, felt, smelled my lion's thought. *Make them fight among themselves, save the cubs.* It wasn't words, but it was emotion that translated into words, because I was human and I needed them. But the idea was good; we had enough power to make them fight among themselves – maybe that could save Micah, and Jason, and Nathaniel? But not yet; I wanted them to call off the first sniper from Micah. I needed to cooperate long enough for them to do that. I told my lioness, *Patience*, and she hunkered down in the long grass and began to wait. She was a stealth predator; they understand patience.

I was out the doors, slipping my sunglasses on against the bright summer sun. I stopped at the top of the steps.

'Keep going,' Nicky said.

'Shouldn't one of you lead, since I don't know which car is yours?'

They exchanged a glance, as if they hadn't thought of it. I had shaken them, or the lioness had. I hoped that would help us. Nicky led the way and Jacob dropped beside me. I'd honestly expected it to be the other way around, but it didn't matter to me.

'I'm cooperating; how about calling your sniper now?'

'When we've searched you for weapons, and we're in the car.'

I let out a breath, nodded, and kept walking. I wanted to scream at them to call off their sniper, but they were recovering from the metaphysical surprise my lion had thrown them. They were gathering their plan around them again, sinking into it. I debated on whether I wanted them back in control. For now, I gained nothing by poking at them, so I followed skater boy to a big SUV. They had parked at the edge of the lot, so that thick trees and bushes were against the far side, so when they took me around to the passenger side, no one could see them frisk me.

'Lean on the truck,' Jacob said.

I put my hands on the side of the very clean SUV. There was a rental sticker in the window. I was thinking again, noticing things again. I could do this. We'd all get out alive, and that thought, that hope, was what they were counting on. Hope is a wonderful thing, but it can be used by very bad people to get you to cooperate until it's too late. You think you'll find a way out until it's too late to save yourself, too late to save others, too late for anything that matters. Serial killers do that a lot, put a weapon on you in a public area, and then make you get into their car, promising not to hurt you. They lie. The general rule is that if someone puts a weapon on you in a busy area where you can yell for help, yell. Because once they get you alone, what they plan to do to you is a lot worse than getting shot, or stabbed, or a quick death. You never let the bad guys run the show, ever. I knew that. I really knew that, but I leaned against the truck and prepared to let them take my weapons. I knew I'd do what they wanted until they made that first call to the sniper on Micah. I had no other options – yet. And that bastard hope made me think I'd have another chance later to do more, even while the other part of me snickered cynically in my brain. I was acting like a civilian, and though I'd never worn a uniform of any kind, civilian was not what I was.

Jacob started patting me down, starting at my wrists under the suit jacket. He paused. 'I can rip the jacket, or you can put your arms back and I can slip it off; your choice.'

I put my arms back, and he slipped the jacket down, surprisingly gently. The jacket revealed the knife sheaths on both forearms with their slender silver-coated daggers. It also showed the shoulder holster against the rich blue of the tank top, and the Smith and Wesson at the small of my back.

'This is what you wear for every day?' Jacob asked.

'Not usually, but I'm expecting a call about a vampire execution out of state.'

'When and from whom?' he asked.

Whom? What kind of bad guy uses *whom*? But I didn't say it out loud; I wanted this to go fast so he'd make that phone call. 'I don't know for sure, and the marshal in charge of the case.'

'That's a custom shoulder rig,' Nicky said.

'My shoulders are narrow enough I have to have custom to fit anyway, so I put on some extras.'

'They aren't narrow; you're just small,' he said.

'Fine, take the weapons, and make the damn call.'

'Some girls just can't take a compliment,' Nicky said, leaning in close enough to put his face against my hair, as his hands found the gun at the small of my back, and pulled it from its holster. He rubbed his cheek against my hair like he was scent-marking me. I think he meant it to be irritating, or maybe even threatening; some women would have taken it that way, but the moment enough of his body touched mine with no cloth, no gloves in between, the power flared between us like a hot wind.

I expected him to pull back, but he didn't, he sort of collapsed around me, hugging me to him with my own gun in his hand. Everywhere we touched the power grew, as if we'd burn if we touched too long. But fire wasn't the right analogy, because it didn't hurt. It felt good.

'Stop it,' I said, and made sure there was anger in the words.

He rubbed his face against mine harder, his lips pressing along my cheek. 'It feels good; I can smell that you think so, too.'

'Get the fuck off me!' But anger wasn't the right thing, either, because my beasts all reacted to anger. I had a moment of those other shadow beasts moving in the dark of me, but the lioness shoved them back. I watched her pull her lips away from those sharp teeth and draw the air into her mouth, scenting over her Jacobson's Organ, so she could literally taste his power on the air.

He had his arms pinning mine, but only above the elbows, so that I could draw one of the knives and start to turn it into his arm. I wasn't thinking about anything but getting him off me. Another hand grabbed mine, knife and all, and more power flared from that hand, too, so that the three of us were suddenly bathed in the power as if we'd all three fallen into a warm bath all at once. Our heads were below the water and we were drowning in the power. My necromancy folded away. It was just gone. It had given me a little more control of the lion in me; now I was bare to the power, to the pull of them.

I heard Jacob say, 'Jesus,' and then his power smashed into all of it and it was like a fist smashing a house of cards. It scattered the power, stripped the energy, and shut down both of them. He tried to shut down my beast, but he couldn't. She snarled at him inside my head, and the sound trickled out my mouth.

He pulled both my blades from their sheaths and threw them on the ground, so he could tear Nicky away from me. Nicky went into a crouch, hands at his sides. He had both my guns in his hands, but he threw them to the ground in the bushes beside the knives so they faced each other bare-handed.

I thought about going for a weapon, but they'd missed the big knife that sat under my hair and down my spine; if they didn't touch me again I wouldn't be unarmed. And I was still too busy trying to control the animal in me to mess with their fight. The lioness's emotions/thoughts were loud in my head. She thought they were strong, and liked it, and wanted to make them fight over us and save our family. I tried to explain to the beast that we needed them alive until they called the sniper, but it was too complex for my lion. I leaned against the truck and concentrated on controlling my breathing, quieting my pulse, and having her hunker back down into the grass. It wasn't time to make our rush; we'd miss our prey. It was too soon; *save your energy for the last big run.* That she understood. Conservation of energy is a very real concept for a predator. We needed to wait for our timing to be just right.

'We are not going to fight over her, Nicky. Remember who you are. Remember what you are.'

Nicky blinked the one eye that wasn't hidden in his skater-cut bangs; it had gone to lion amber. He growled at his friend.

'Nicky, we're on a job.'

Nicky closed his eyes, fists at his side. He hugged himself tight. 'Your eyes have changed, Jacob. Your fucking eyes shifted.'

The words made me look at the other man's face and see him blinking pale yellow eyes. His own eyes had been a pale enough gray that it hadn't been as obvious as Nicky's eyes going from blue to amber. They both almost shifted. Lycanthropes as powerful as they were didn't lose control in a public parking lot; they just didn't.

Jacob turned those lion eyes toward me, his human face holding them like they belonged, or maybe I'd just spent too much time looking at Micah's leopard eyes to think it was weird. 'You're in heat.'

I shook my head. 'I don't know what you mean by that.'

'Yeah, you do,' he said, voice getting quieter, more controlled. He bent to pick up the guns and said, 'Take off the arm sheaths so we can put the blades in them. If you do what the client wants, you get it all back at the end of the night.'

I honestly didn't know what it meant for a werelion to be in heat, but I didn't debate with him, just started unbuckling the wrist sheaths. 'Call your sniper off. It's not my fault that we've been delayed.'

He nodded, shoving one of the guns into his waistband and handing the other to Nicky, who took it and tucked it out of sight under the baggy tank top. Jacob got his cell phone out and called. 'Stand down for now. She's cooperating.' Silence. 'Yes, keep on him, but just observe.' He looked at me; his eyes had gone back to human gray. 'I know you don't have complete control when you're in heat, but if you do that again in an enclosed space like a car, we won't make our deadlines. That means that the next call that I need to make to the snipers on your men might not get made in time. Do you understand that?'

'You're saying that you both might forget your job and we'd just fuck our way through the deadlines while my boyfriends died.'

'That's exactly what I'm saying, so it's in everyone's best interest if you keep a lid on it.'

'I will do my best,' I said, and meant it. I handed him one of the knife sheaths. We were both careful not to touch bare skin to bare skin as he took it from me.

'Look at me,' Nicky said.

'Don't push at this,' Jacob said.

'Lions are weird about weaknesses; I just want her to see. Maybe if her beast knows, she won't want me anymore and the power won't turn into a fight between us.'

Jacob nodded. 'Good idea.'

'What's a good idea?' I asked.

Nicky lifted that long fall of blond bangs away from the right side of his face. His right eye was missing. Burn scars traced over the empty socket, caressed the edge of his cheek, and covered where his right eyebrow should have been. I looked because he seemed to want me to. I didn't look away because I was sharing my bed with a vampire that made Nicky's scar look like child's play, though the whole eye destroyed was worse. Asher had all the parts he was supposed to have; just some of them were nestled in burn scars.

Nicky blinked the one big blue eye at me, then let the hair fall back into place, and just like that it was hidden. 'Most women, especially women, look disgusted or scared. You don't look either.'

I shrugged. 'If you know everyone in my bed then you know scars aren't a deal breaker for me.'

'You mean the vampire with the holy water scars,' he said. I nodded.

He seemed to think about that for a few seconds, then nodded. 'Guess you've seen worse.'

'It's not about worse, Nicky; it's about the fact that the scar is just another part of you. Not bad, not good, just you.' I held my left arm out so the flat of the arm showed. I pointed to the mound of scar tissue at the bend. 'Vampire.' I touched the claw marks next. 'Shapeshifted witch.' I traced the knife wound that made the cross-shaped burn scar a little crooked now. 'Knife and burn were both human servants of different master vampires.' I touched the flat, slick scar on the upper part of the arm. 'Bad guy's girlfriend shot me.' If I hadn't been afraid I'd flash the knife sheath under my tank top, I'd have showed him my collarbone scar. 'I've got a few others, but we'd have to be better friends for me to show you those.'

He studied my face. 'Most werelion females don't want a one-eyed mate.'

'It's an old scar,' I said. 'I'm assuming you've compensated by now.'

He nodded. 'But I've got a blind side in both forms; it's a problem in a fight.'

'I fight my own battles most of the time.'

He grinned. 'Which is why you don't have a mate yet, and why your lioness is in heat. If you'd picked a mate, it wouldn't have happened.'

I would talk to our local lions about leaving that part out, but in their defense I wouldn't have believed them. I'd have just thought it was Haven trying to get back in my pants after the fight we had. No, I couldn't blame this on them.

'It's not just heat,' Jacob said, 'it's fucking powerful heat. No female has ever made me lose it like that.'

'So neither of you has mates, either,' I said.

'She's right, it's not just her being picky that made this happen.'

'It's said a man of a certain age and property is in want of a wife,' I said.

'Did you just quote *Pride and Prejudice*?' Jacob asked.

'I guess I did, embarrassing, sorry.'

'I wouldn't have known what book, or who you quoted,' Nicky said, not like he was happy with it.

'But I get what you mean with the quote,' Jacob said; 'my hair is starting to gray and I've never taken a real mate. I've never committed to a territory and my pride is all males, except for one, and she's not into guys, so it's not a problem.'

'We travel too much for women and kids,' Nicky said.

Jacob nodded. 'That's what I keep telling myself. Now get in the car, Anita. We've still got a job to do. Remember what I said about controlling your side of the problem. Nothing we could do would be worth the lives of your lovers.'

'Agreed,' I said.

He handed me my jacket. I slipped it back over the empty shoulder rig, but still had the big knife down my spine. He held the passenger door for me, and I didn't protest the gallantry, though under the circumstances it seemed weirder than normal. Nicky got in behind me and leaned against the back of my seat. 'I wish you weren't the job, Anita.'

'Me, too,' I said, and meant it, though probably not for the same reason he did.

Jacob got in behind the wheel and said, 'Buckle up; it'll slow you down by a few seconds if you decide to do something stupid.'

I buckled up. 'So we go on with your plan?'

'Yes,' he said, 'nothing's changed.'

'So you'll still kill the people I love if I don't raise the dead for your client?'

'Yes,' he said.

'Yes,' Nicky said from behind me.

'Then we're clear,' I said.

Jacob started the engine. 'Yeah, we're clear. You'll kill us if you can, and if you're sure it won't get your people killed. We'll kill you if you force us to.'

'Great,' I said, 'we all know the rules then.'

'Why aren't you afraid?' Nicky whispered from behind me.

'Being afraid won't help.'

'People are brave, but you can always smell the fear, taste their heart speed up. But you aren't. You really aren't any of that.'

'If I get afraid, or pissed, then my pulse rises, and my heart races, and my blood pressure goes up and it's harder to control the beasts. Jacob was clear; I can't afford to lose control in the car with you guys.'

'So because you have to be in control, you will be, just like that,' he said.

'Just like that,' I said, and watched where Jacob drove so if I lived through the night I could take the police back to their client and arrest his, or her, ass.

'If I'd known what you were we might not have taken the job,' Jacob said.

'Nice thought, but it doesn't really help us out, does it?'

'No, we took the client's money, we have to deliver.'

'Then it doesn't matter to me if you feel guilty or not, Jacob. In fact, I think it's worse that you're going to maybe kill the people I love, the people that make up my pride, and maybe kill me, and you'll regret it, but you'll do it anyway. That's not honor, Jacob, that's your conscience letting you know that you're doing the wrong thing.'

'It's not my conscience, Anita, it's my libido, my beast, and it doesn't have a conscience.'

He was right on that, but I also knew that wereanimals aren't just animals. There is a person in there and there is a conscience. The beast usually didn't care about it, and could make you do terrible things that you had trouble living with afterward, but this time Jacob and Nicky's beasts were on the same side as their conscience. It made me hopeful, and I cursed it, because hope will keep you alive, yes, but it will also get you killed in ways worse than anything you can imagine. Hope is a bad friend when men with guns have you. But my lioness and their lions lusted after each other, sort of. Lust I trusted. Hope will lie to you, but lust is what it is; it never lies. Hope would keep me hoping, but lust might be a weapon I could use to divide them. Divide and conquer has been a strategy for thousands of years; there's a reason for that.

WE DROVE TO a very nice subdivision in a part of St Louis where the yards are large, the houses larger. Some of the smaller yards had the biggest houses, as if the owners felt insecure and had to compensate for something. The driveway we finally pulled into was long and swept gracefully from the road to a house that was as big as any and had one of the largest yards I'd seen. From house to professionally landscaped yard the place breathed money and care, and didn't seem to feel it needed to compensate for anything. The whole image was so perfect you knew the architect had worked with the landscaper to make the visuals, as if a magazine photographer should pop out of the shrubbery and put it all on the cover.

'You don't smell surprised,' Nicky said, as we all got out of their rental.

I just shrugged.

Jacob blocked my way up the driveway. He studied my face. 'Did you know the client's address before we drove you here?'

'No.'

'Are you lying?' he asked.

I frowned at him. 'No, I don't know who your client is, and I didn't know you'd bring me to one of our nicer new-money neighborhoods. But I did know it had to be someone with enough money to afford your kind of help.' The moment I said it, I was betting on Natalie Zell. Any woman who wanted to raise her own husband from the dead so she could chop him up with an axe then bury the pieces 'alive' wouldn't blink at a little kidnapping and the deaths of men she didn't even know.

I heard Nicky close behind me and fought not to move out from between them. I never liked for my kidnappers to flank me, and really didn't like shapeshifters this close when they meant me harm. 'You're crowding me, Nicky.'

'She smells like the truth,' he said, but was still too close.

Jacob nodded, but said, 'Give her some room, Nicky; we don't want to accidentally touch each other.'

He backed up a few steps, so that I followed Jacob's broad back with Nicky trailing us. There was no talking, no questions; we just went for the front door. Nice that the client didn't make us use the servants' entrance. Did mansions have servants' entrances these days?

'No questions,' Nicky said.

'No,' I said.

'Most people would have questions, especially women. They always talk too much.'

Jacob rang a doorbell that made a rich, melodious sound deep inside the house.

'You make a habit of kidnapping women?'

'Work is work,' he said.

'Sure,' I said. We waited to the tune of birdsong and someone's lawn service in the distance using a large mower.

'They talk because they're nervous,' he said.

'The only one talking is you, Nicky,' I said.

'I'm not nervous,' he said, but it was too quick a denial, and there was a tone in his voice.

'Liar,' I said, softly.

'Drop it, Nicky,' Jacob said. He straightened his shoulders just a bit, and I knew he'd heard something I hadn't. A moment later the door opened and I was left staring at Tony Bennington.

Now I was surprised. 'Son of a bitch,' I said. He'd seemed so much more sane than Natalie Zell. Just another grief-stricken husband trying to bargain with God to get his wife back, but I guess when God didn't listen he'd bargained with someone else, something a little lower than heaven. When God ignores you, the devil starts looking good.

'That's better,' Nicky said. 'You really didn't know.' But he said it soft from behind me and I'm not sure that the 'client' heard him. I didn't give a damn if he did.

'Welcome to my home, Ms Blake.' He actually did that arm-sweeping gesture to invite us all inside. I fought a really serious urge to punch him in the jaw.

Nicky grabbed my right arm; my jacket and his gloves kept us from touching bare skin, but his grip was firm. He leaned in and whispered, 'Hitting the client won't help.'

'You saw me tense,' I whispered back.

'Yep.'

I started to protest that I wasn't really going to hit Bennington, but I wasn't sure it was the truth. I wanted to hurt him; I really did. Apparently all the nerves and fear that I wasn't letting myself feel were going to translate into violence. Goody, that fucking worked for me.

Of course, with my anger the lioness started to creep forward in the metaphorical grass she was crouched in. I had to close my eyes and concentrate on my breathing. In, out, slow, steady; control the breathing and you control the emotion. When I thought I could look at Bennington without wanting to hit him, I opened my eyes.

He was looking at me, his gray eyes uncertain, like someone who had purchased a dog but hadn't done their research, and now the dog was trying to eat the cat.

'I understand your anger with me, Ms Blake. I am truly sorry it had to come to this.'

It was an echo of what I'd told him in my office. I was truly sorry for his loss; truly sorry I couldn't help him. The echo didn't help me keep the anger down; it flared again, and I felt Nicky's hand tighten on my arm again. It helped remind me that my control was all that stood between my lovers and a sniper's bullet. I had to hold it together for them.

'You want me to raise your wife as a zombie,' I said, and my voice was utterly empty. I'd started to fold away inside myself, going to that quiet place I went to when I killed someone not in a firefight, but when I stared down the barrel of a gun and pulled the trigger with thought and time to change my mind. It was the quiet inside my head when I had decided to take a life even if there was opportunity to save it. When I had decided that someone deserved to die, and my conscience was clear. I had one of those moments now, and it helped chase back the heat of the lions. It was a cold place, the place I went when I killed.

I pictured Bennington dead with my bullet in his forehead and it gave me comfort. It helped me smile and be calm.

Nicky let go of me. 'She's calm.'

'Yeah,' Jacob said, 'calm the way Silas gets.' He was studying my face, and it wasn't metaphysical abilities that let him understand my expression and the peacefulness in my eyes.

'You're comparing her to Silas,' Nicky said. 'Shit.'

I didn't know who Silas was, and I didn't care. I probably should have, but I didn't. I forced myself to see the room beyond Bennington's face. When in danger, exits and entryways become important. The room was white: white carpet, white leather furniture, a slightly different shade of white wall. It was like they hadn't been able to decide on a color so they didn't choose one. The only color in that white room was a life-size portrait of Bennington's wife. She was still blond and beautiful, but the photograph showed that she was model thin, which meant too thin for my tastes, but no one had asked me. She was wearing a bright blue ankle-length dress that made her eyes a brilliant blue. She lounged on a rattan couch that was surrounded by lush tropical plants, some of them in crimson and pink blooms. It was the only color in all that whiteness. It loomed over the room like some kind of goddess on high, or maybe a shrine. Jesus.

As for the exits, there were huge glass doors on one side of the fireplace, and more of them scattered throughout the bottom half of the open great room. There was one hallway that led deeper into the downstairs, and a huge-ass staircase leading up.

Nicky leaned in and whispered, 'Don't bother scouting the room, Anita.'

I didn't even look at him, as if I didn't know what he was

talking about, but I didn't like how alert both lions were to my actions. It was going to limit my chances.

'Did your man acquire what we need for tonight?' Bennington asked, looking at Jacob.

'Silas will.'

'I'm paying you a great deal of money, Mr Leon.'

I decided to go for smart-ass; when in doubt, it's always a possibility. 'Leon,' I said, 'that is so not your real last name.'

He gave me an unfriendly look out of his pale eyes.

I smiled at him, able to do it because I'd calmed myself with images of violence. It had emptied my mind enough to scout the room, and to think. It's not a technique that they teach you in business school, but it works for me.

'It's my name today.'

'What's wrong with Leon as his name?' Bennington asked.

'It's based on the Latin word *leo*, which means "lion." Don't you think that's funny? Because I think it's freaking hilarious.'

'I think I liked it better when you weren't talking,' Jacob said.

'They come highly recommended, Ms Blake.'

'You've had them watching me and my boyfriends for a few days, before you came to my office. You hired them before I turned you down.' The anger tried to flare back up, and I had to slow my breathing a little, concentrate on my pulse. I pictured him dead again, but the anger wanted him dead sooner, and that was the beast talking. *Kill it now, eat it now, why wait?* Animals are very into instant gratification.

'I told you, Ms Blake, I'd researched you. Everything I had learned about you said that you would turn me down, so I had a contingency in place.'

'A contingency. Is that what they're calling kidnapping and murder for hire these days?'

He flinched a little around his eyes, as if it were all too blunt for his sensibilities. 'I'm truly hoping it doesn't come to that, Ms Blake. If you raise my wife for me, then no harm comes to the men you love. You go back to your life and I go back to mine.'

I looked at Jacob. 'He may be an amateur, but you aren't. How are you going to make it safe for us all to go back to our lives?'

'Why don't we all sit down,' he said.

Bennington stammered, 'Of course, of course, how rude of me, I mean . . .' He trailed off as if he'd just heard himself, or didn't know how to finish the sentence.

'Always hard to know how polite to be to your victims, isn't it, Tony?'

'Sit down, Anita,' Jacob said, and his tone implied that if I didn't sit down, he'd help me do it.

'She's tensed up again. She wants to fight. We can't afford to posture, Jacob,' Nicky said.

It was Jacob's turn to count to ten.

'Am I missing something?' Bennington said.

'Loads,' I said, smiling sweetly.

'Let's all sit down and discuss how we're going to live through this,' Jacob said in a voice that was reasonable, even pleasant. I wondered what visual he used to gain control. Had he pictured injuring me, killing me?

But we all sat down in the huge great room that most modern houses have for living rooms. I don't like them, they're too open. They are absolutely indefensible and seemed designed to make a burglar's job easier. This room was particularly so, with the large stairway sweeping up one side with an open-railed hallway that cut across the entire length of the huge space. With all the talk of snipers it made me particularly not happy with the floor plan. I knew no one was up there, but it was just not a comfortable room when you knew that people really were out to get you. Of course, the people out to get me were sitting down on the white leather furniture looking at me. There was the mysterious Silas and his errand that he hadn't finished, but right now there were enough enemies in front of me; I didn't have to borrow.

'We're just going to wait here until Silas phones, and then we'll pack up and head for the cemetery,' Jacob said.

Bennington added, 'I had her reburied because I found that most animators needed a grave rather than a mausoleum.'

'Very thoughtful,' I said, and didn't try to keep the anger out of my voice.

'I am being reasonable, Ms Blake. I could have had them kill your first boyfriend, Callahan, as an incentive for cooperation. You, unlike me, have spares.'

'They're people, not extra tires in case of emergency.' The anger rose another notch, and I had to control my breathing again, count again. The lioness was getting impatient in the long grass. *We could kill him before they could stop us.* She was probably right, and if we killed him then the money went away. That was an interesting idea.

'You've thought of something, Anita. I can see it in the set of your shoulders, the way you went still. Whatever it is, don't do it,' Jacob said.

The trouble with wereanimals that were also professional

bad guys was that it's very hard to surprise them. The only way to do it was to take action before you really think about it, the way you do in martial arts. You see your opening and you react, because you've already made your decision to hurt them before the fight starts. If I killed Bennington, would they be professional and just stop all this, or would they kill at least one of my lovers as an object lesson? Until I had an answer to that question, did I dare kill Bennington if the chance came?

Jacob sat down on the couch beside me, arm on the back of it, like we were a couple. I leaned just out of touching of the arm. He could think I was being unfriendly, but I didn't want him to feel the knife hilt under my shirt. Thanks to the lions being overly friendly I had one weapon left; I didn't want to lose it.

He leaned in and spoke low. 'Whatever you are thinking, it won't work. We have a sniper on all three of them. They'll call in as each man goes outside for the first time today. They'll follow them and if we don't call in periodically, they'll kill them.'

'I understand that,' I said, but part of me filed away the fact that he'd said *we*. Jacob didn't have to be the one to make the phone calls to the shooters. Nicky could do it. I only needed one of them alive and on my side. I tried to breathe past the anger and that edge of fear that wanted to scream through me. I had to think, which meant neither anger nor fear was my friend. Fear will keep you alive, and anger will help you in a fight sometimes, but when it came to planning action you needed no emotions. Be empty, be still, and think.

'I am sorry, Ms Blake, to force you, but I want the woman I love back, you understand that.'

'I'll do my best, but it will still only be a zombie. No matter how lifelike she looks when you first see her, it can't last, Mr Bennington.'

'I've been told that there is one set of circumstances where the recently dead can be raised as a zombie but stay intact.'

'If so, it's news to me.' I was leaning forward a little, trying not to let Jacob touch me. For some reason that made him move closer to me so that our hips touched on the couch. Great, it was like one of those dates where the guy doesn't respect your personal space.

'Mr Bennington,' Jacob said, 'I wouldn't overshare with Anita. She's cooperating, and once Silas does his part we'll head to the gravesite. We don't need to talk about the details.'

Then Bennington gave me a look. It was hostile. 'You know, I wasn't certain I could go through with it. I actually thought I might lose the first half of the payment and not do this, but then I saw the pictures of your lunch with your lovers. I watched your Mr Schuyler and your Mr Graison flirt. My Ilsa liked to flirt; in fact, she loved it. She loved attention and she had a fascination with shapeshifters.'

So he knew she was a fur-fucker. I just looked at him, not sure what emotion he wanted from me. I gave him a blank face and waited for him to talk. He was in that villain speech mode that only the amateurs do.

'I watched them comfort you, and then watched you flirt with the waiter. You wouldn't give me back my flirt, so I took yours, and if you take my Ilsa away from me again, I will take your men away from you forever.'

I must have tensed forward, not on purpose, because Jacob put his arm across my shoulders just in case, but I'd been too intent on Bennington's words. I'd forgotten for a second that I didn't want him to touch my back.

I tried to stand up, and he grabbed me, but I managed to get to my feet, but Nicky was there behind me, arms hugging me from behind, and this time he wasn't distracted by lion hormones. 'What the hell is that?'

'Something big that you missed,' Jacob said.

I forced myself not to struggle in Nicky's grip, but I couldn't not tense up, or stop the lioness from not wanting them to manhandle her, us. I had a moment of pronoun loss, and that growl trickled out from between my lipsticked lips. Heat came with it in a rush over my skin like a sudden fever. I was suddenly so hot, so hot, but I wasn't sweating.

'Her skin is hot to the touch,' Nicky said, and his voice sounded strangled, as if he were fighting off his own growl.

'I can feel the energy,' Jacob said.

Bennington stood up, got close to me, trusting Nicky to keep me from hurting him. Nicky tightened his arms around my body, pinning my arms to my sides. He held on tight enough that it was almost hard to breathe. 'You wanted to know what our plan is for us to go back to our lives; well, you will use the energy of a human sacrifice to raise Ilsa from the dead. It will be enough energy to make her beautiful forever, mine forever. And once you use murder to raise the dead, you can't tell on us without risking the death penalty yourself.'

I found my voice. 'That's the errand that Silas is supposed to finish, isn't it?'

Nicky tightened his grip until it dug my empty holster into my body, and it began to truly hurt, but I didn't mind; the pain helped me think. It helped me not give in to the snarling lion inside me. If we killed Bennington, the second half of their money was gone. And they were professionals. I didn't think they'd kill us for free. It was a plan, and besides, we wanted him dead. It's hard to fight the inner beast when you agree with it.

The lioness charged out of that long metaphysical or metaphorical grass, and began to run full out up that path inside me. She was a golden blur, moving through me.

'Fight it,' Nicky said in my ear.

I glared at Bennington. 'Why?'

Jacob was in front of me, blocking my view of Bennington. 'Because if you shift, you can't raise the dead and you're no good to us. Don't make us kill you, Anita.'

Nicky spoke through gritted teeth as if it were beginning to be an effort to hold me. 'Don't make us kill your men.'

'Look at me, Anita!'

But all I could see was that blur of gold, and for the first time I didn't want to put a wall between her and me. For the first time I needed the help, and I would take it.

Jacob grabbed my face, forced me to look at him, but he also touched bare skin to bare skin. I snarled up at him, and the golden blur slowed. Slowed and screamed through me, so that my body vibrated with the sound of her rage, her need, her hunger.

'God, she smells good,' Nicky said.

'Don't you start,' Jacob said, but he was still touching my face, and the look in his eyes was uncertain, as if he were listening to things I couldn't hear. His lion was talking to him, too. Would it help me to force them to change?

Jacob said, 'Get out, Bennington, get out until we call you. She's not safe.'

The lioness screamed again, and the sound came out of my throat. It hurt, as if the sound needed a bigger throat, a different mouth, and it rubbed raw things that should never have held the sound.

Jacob had a look on his face, a lost look. 'Maybe you can bring our beasts, but if you do we'll fall on each other and either fight over you, or both fuck you. Either way we might not hear the other phone calls. We might miss calling off our shooters on your other men. They might kill them not because we want them to, but because we missed the call.'

Nicky breathed against my hair, 'Put your beast in the deep freeze, Anita, please.' He was holding me tight enough that I knew his body was happy to be pressed against mine. He meant the *please*.

My skin felt so hot, but it didn't feel bad like a fever; it felt wonderful. Part of me wondered what it might be like to finally give in and shift, but not today. I couldn't afford to think that today.

Jacob's phone started ringing as if on cue. He looked at me. 'I have to get this, and you have to regain your control.' He kept his grip on my face, but used his other hand to get his phone out of his pocket.

He watched my face like he'd memorize it, but spoke: 'Stand down, just follow and observe.' He started to put the phone away, but it rang again. 'Yeah, no, just observe, just follow. Stand down until further orders.'

I realized that was three calls. All of them were safe unless Jacob called back and told them to shoot them. Him dead or unable to phone would fix that.

'Chill,' Nicky said, 'chill, damn it.' His words made sense, but he was starting to nuzzle my hair. The lioness had slowed and was sniffing the air. I ground my hips into Nicky just a little bit. He made a soft wordless sound.

'Shit,' Jacob said. He moved his free hand along my neck until he found the hilt of the big knife under my hair and jacket. He got a handful of my hair, moving it out of the way as he drew the knife out. Nicky moved back enough for him to do it. The size of the blade put more of a damper on their amour than anything I could have done.

Jacob held it up to the light. It gleamed, and the edge was as sharp as it looked. 'This is as big as her forearm; how the fuck did you miss it?'

Nicky blinked up at the blade. 'I was searching her when the lioness did its thing. My bad.'

Jacob sighed, and lowered the blade. I couldn't read the look on his face. It was partly sad and partly something else. 'It's okay, Nicky. You've never been around a Regina when she's in heat. A pride can tear itself apart before she picks a mate.'

The lioness rolled onto her back, rolling on the ground like any cat. It made me writhe against Nicky, and he didn't exactly fight the sensation. I was going to lose control, and sex would be the least of what we might do. I tried to think.

'My first pride died that way, because the Regina wanted the strongest Rex, so she waited for the winner. I promised myself I would keep my men away from shit like that.'

Nicky changed his grip, letting me have my arms, picking me up around the waist, lifting me off the ground. My hands went to his arm, holding on, but not fighting. I was out of weapons. What would help me? What would help me stop them? I mean, I was good at sex, or so the men in my life told me, but good enough to make them turn down a shitload of money and betray their other men? I wasn't that good. No one was that good. If sex wouldn't help me, I had to stop what was happening. Chill, he had said. I tried to call my necromancy, like I had in the restaurant, but the lion was too loud in my head. I could smell lion. I think it was Nicky, but it was as if the world were drowning in the thick musk of it. I couldn't breathe past it. I didn't want cold blood, I wanted hot.

Nicky collapsed onto the leather couch with me under him. The height difference meant that he wasn't lined up for anything, but his hands slipped under my skirt, and I struggled out from under him, spilling myself to the carpet. Nicky stayed on the couch, staring at me with one wide eye, his breathing labored.

I crawled backward away from him, and he let me, but I'd forgotten about the other lion. It was too careless for words, but I wasn't thinking clearly. The lioness was eating what made me *me*. I understood in that moment that I didn't have to shift to lose myself. I crawled into Jacob's legs and started forward, but he reached down, grabbed my arms, and pulled me to my feet. I was suddenly staring into his face from inches away as he bent that tall body down to me. He said, 'Oh, God.' It was more a cry for help than a sound of passion.

I felt his other arm move and went to block it without thinking. My hand traced down his arm to find my knife. 'Is this really what you want to stick in me, Jacob?'

He swallowed so hard it sounded painful. 'Don't do this.'

'You first,' I whispered.

'What?'

'Call off your cats, don't earn the second half of Bennington's money.'

He shook his head. 'You aren't my queen yet.'

Nicky came behind me, hands sliding over my back. Jacob growled at him, but the younger man said, 'We don't have to fight. She shares just fine.' He ground himself into me from behind, shoving me against Jacob. I was suddenly held between both of them, and they were both hard and ready. I couldn't help but react to it, writhing between the two of them. It was Jacob who pulled me back from the other man, and said, 'I'm Rex of this pride. I don't share.'

'That's what destroyed your first pride,' Nicky said. 'Didn't you learn anything from that?'

'I learned that if you are king, then be king.' He kissed me, hard and fierce, so that I had to open my mouth, let him inside, or he'd have cut my lips on my teeth. He was all hands and mouth and need. My lioness didn't like him. She snarled inside my head. He didn't share; the pride was all about sharing. My life was all about sharing. The group mattered more than anything else. The group had to survive.

I pushed him back enough to break the kiss. I snarled into his face. 'I rule myself! I don't need another king.'

Something crashed into him, and I had a breath to realize it was Nicky, and then they were rolling on the ground fighting for real. I didn't stay to watch. Jacob had dropped my big blade. I picked it up and ran for the door that Bennington had gone through. If he died, the job died with him. That worked for me.

A lion roared behind me, and I didn't look back to see who

it was, but I used the speed that my beasts had given me and ran. I had the speed but not all the senses, so I had a second before the door opened and I was staring at a tall, dark-haired man. He smelled like lion. The blade struck out in a blur of silver. Action was so far ahead of thought that I had sliced him from ribs to belt, and was starting to bring the knife back for a second blow, as his fist struck out at me. I was able to move back a little, but the speed was too much, and I was too committed to moving forward. His fist blurred out and hit me in the face. It was like being hit by a baseball bat: pressure, momentum, no pain, just a stop. The inside of my head just stopped like my brain had run into a wall. There wasn't even time to think, *Oh, he hit me*. It was just the blow and I was down. The lights went out and so did I.

THE FIRST SENSATION I had was of bare dirt under my hands. The ground was cool against the backs of my thighs through the hose. I could feel walls around me, that enclosed feeling, but there was a thread of wind as if there were a window open somewhere. The wind smelled of trees and grass. The dirt smelled fresh and cool. A few night insects called, sluggish in the unusually cool summer temperatures. I drew in a bigger breath, and smelled soap and aftershave, and under that the nose-tickling scent of lion. That made me open my eyes to the sloping roof of a shed. The window above me was partially broken, and there were plenty of gaps between the boards on the walls, so the wind eased through at will. I heard the wind in tall trees high above us. It was blowing harder higher up. I'd expected whatever werelion was guarding me to say something, but I had to turn my head slowly to find Nicky sitting beside me in the dark. He had his knees drawn up to his chest, hugging them, his cheek resting on them so his good eye could see me. The moon was bright enough through the broken windows to let me see him clearly. The brightness of it reminded me that it was only two days until full moon. That might have been one reason they had so much trouble with my beast. The closer to full moon, the harder it was to control your beast.

Nicky gave a small smile. 'Good, you're not dead.'

'Was I supposed to be?' I asked.

'When Silas hit you and you dropped like that –' he shrugged – 'it was a thought.'

'I didn't even have time to worry about it. He was so fast.'

'You managed to move a little out of the way or he'd have snapped your neck.'

I started to try to get up, but he touched my arm. 'Stay down a little longer. Once you get up, then you have to raise the dead.'

'Did you win the fight with Jacob?'

'You nearly dying sort of stopped it.' He grinned, a sudden whiteness in the dark. 'And we had to help patch up Silas. You opened him up from' – he sat up so he could use his own body to demonstrate – 'here at just under the ribs, across the stomach, to the upper intestine. I got to see his intestines on the outside. That is one sharp blade.'

I heard footsteps rustling the leaves, and the crooked door opened to show a dark shadow that turned out to be Jacob. 'It wasn't just the blade, Nick. She knows how to use a knife.' Apparently he'd heard us, too. He walked across the dirt floor and stood on the other side of me, looming over us both. I didn't like that, so I tried to sit up.

'Slowly,' Nicky said, 'you've been mostly dead all night.'

I stopped in midmotion. 'Did you just quote *Princess Bride*?'

'I may not be able to quote books, but movies, those I can do.'

'He's right, though,' Jacob said, and he reached down to offer a hand, 'move slow; there's no way to tell how much you've healed.'

I thought about not taking the hand, but I still needed to get out of this with all my people alive, which meant friendly was still better than unfriendly. His hand closed over mine and it was just a hand. He'd shut down his shields on his power so tight that nothing leaked out. When you're as powerful as he was, that's a lot of shielding. The less powerful, or the newbies, will leak faster, and leak more the closer to the full moon it gets. For Jacob it was just hard to hide that much light under your bushel basket. He lifted me gently to a sitting position. The world stayed steady, but a headache started on the right side of my face from jaw to temple, as if it had waited for me to sit up.

Jacob knelt on one knee beside me, still holding my hand. 'How does it feel?'

'My head and face hurt, but honestly I'm surprised that it's not worse. Aspirin would be great.'

'No, just in case you're bleeding inside your skull you don't want something that thins your blood.' He took his hand back and I let him. 'You seem steady enough. Sit here for a few minutes, and then Nick will help you try standing. I'll go comfort our client again.' He sounded disgusted, but he walked out, having to lift the crooked door to close it behind him. It still left an outline of moonlight on almost every side of it. The shed was so old that I could have torn out a board from the backside and gotten out; maybe Nicky was in here with me to see that I didn't do that very thing.

'Where are we?' I asked.

'In an old shed,' he said.

I gave him the look the comment deserved. It made him smile. 'You know what I meant, Nicky.'

'I think this used to be the caretaker's shed, but now it's a place to hide you out of sight, until you're well enough to raise the dead.'

I took in a deeper breath and realized I could smell old marble. I'd been around it most of my adult life, and it actually did have an odor, if you were close enough to it, or surrounded by enough of it. 'I take it this is the cemetery where Ilsa Bennington is buried.'

'How do you know we're in a cemetery?'

I thought about lying, but decided to save my lies for later. 'I can smell the marble headstones.'

He drew in a deep breath. 'I can, too, but I wasn't sure you could. You don't shift, or that's what we're told.'

'Not yet,' I said.

'Why say it that way?'

I shrugged. 'There's always the chance that my body will complete the change someday. My situation is too rare to really know what will happen in the long run. So, is this where Ilsa is buried?'

'Yep, he found an old, out-of-the-way one so we wouldn't be interrupted.'

'Yeah, without the right permits you can get arrested for disturbance of a corpse, or worse.' I turned my head, and the ache intensified as if some of the muscles or ligaments were bruised. Since I should have been dead, I was okay with that. Jean-Claude's vampire marks had made me damn hard to kill. The thought made me realize that it was after dark and I could contact him by thought alone.

'You won't be able to use metaphysics to contact your vampire master, or anyone else, Anita.' It was almost as if he'd read my thought, though I was pretty sure it was only coincidence.

'I didn't . . .' I said.

'You were stronger metaphysically than we planned, so Jacob called in our team witch. She's done something so that while you're on this land you won't be able to contact anyone mind to mind.'

'What if they try to contact me?'

He shook his head. 'Nope, Ellen is good, and very thorough, and we're also over two hours outside your city. Even if your guys break through, they'll never be able to get to you in time to stop Jacob from telling the snipers to finish the job.'

It was my turn to try to tell if he was lying. I took a deep breath of the cool, earthy air, and there was nothing. He was as peaceful and empty as a still pool of water. It was strangely Zen, and very unlike most of the shapeshifters I knew.

'Besides, if Jacob or Ellen senses you trying to break through the barrier she's put up, then Micah Callahan dies.' He said it with almost no change in inflection, and only the smallest speed of pulse.

My stomach clenched tight at that lack of inflection. It seemed worse that it didn't bother him to talk about destroying someone I loved, someone who was a linchpin on which my happiness revolved. That it didn't matter to him both helped and hurt. It hurt because lack of emotion can make people harder to manipulate, and helped because it made me calmer, made me understand the rules, or lack of them. I could play this game.

I fought the urge to search for the barrier the witch had put up, the same way I'd try a locked door, just in case. If this Ellen was any good at all, she'd sense me trying her barrier. I couldn't risk what her reaction would be; if it had been a real door I could probably have rattled it a little without my 'guards' getting upset, but how do you rattle a metaphysical barrier just a little? My powers tended to rely on brute force more than subtlety. I couldn't risk it. I couldn't risk Micah like that. My voice came out steady; point for me. 'Not that I'm complaining exactly, but why do you keep threatening to kill him first?'

'He's just your Nimir-Raj; the others are your animals to call. We aren't sure exactly what powers you've gained from your vampire master, but if you are some kind of lesser vampire, then killing a wereanimal that you've bound to yourself can sometimes kill you both. We need you alive to raise the zombie, so Micah goes first.'

'If they die . . .'

'Yeah, yeah, you'll kill us all. I know.'

'Did I talk while I was unconscious?'

'No, but we know your rep, and if we kill someone you love there's no going back, no more being friends.' He gave me a very direct look, ruined only by the fall of his pale bangs over the one side of his face. It gave him a perpetually young, frivolous glance, as if nothing that came out of that haircut could be serious. But the weight of his one eye, the face I could see, was very serious.

'If you have to kill Micah then you'll kill me, too, because you know if you don't I'll hunt you down.'

'Yeah, Jacob doesn't want to kill you for a lot of reasons,

but he understands that if certain lines are crossed he'll have no choice.' He leaned against the wall of the shed. 'The wood's solid even with all the cracks,' he said.

'Solid or not, it's not exactly a secure prison for me. Why are we in here?'

His hands were looser on his knees as he said, 'Jacob's afraid you've rolled me like a real vampire. I've never challenged him before, Anita, never. I've been with his pride since I was nineteen, and I've never challenged him. I want to touch you. I mean, you're beautiful and all, but this is more than that. My fingertips tingle with the need to hold you. What did you do to me?'

I was calm only on the surface; underneath was that bubbling fear. He might not be able to tell I was lying by smell or body language, but why lie when the truth will do? 'I'm not entirely sure.'

He studied me, head resting on his knees. 'I don't believe you.'

'You could tell if I was lying earlier; can't you tell now?'

'Your pulse sped up when I talked about killing your Nimir-Raj, and you're scared for him, so, no, I can't tell.' He frowned and shifted uneasily on the cool dirt. 'Why did I tell you that? I should have just kept saying I didn't believe you, and I definitely shouldn't have offered so much information. Why did I do that?'

'I told the truth, Nicky; I don't know.'

'You could be lying,' he said.

'I could,' I said, 'but you'll just have to take it on faith that I'm not.'

He gave me a look that even in the dimness of the shed

was clear. It was a look that said he didn't take anything on faith. He gave a sound halfway between a laugh and a snort. He was still smiling as he said, 'What have you done to me, Anita?'

'I don't know,' I said, and my body was growing even calmer, because no one was actively trying to hurt me or mine, and I needed to save some of the adrenaline for later. It wasn't really a conscious thing; just if the violence wasn't immediate, I calmed.

His smile began to slip away as he asked, 'But if you had to guess, what would it be?'

'Touch me and maybe we'll figure it out.' That was true, touch would help me understand what was happening more, but I was still trying to find an ally in all this mess. I needed help, and he'd sense if I called anyone mind to mind, which left him as the best chance I had for help.

He hugged his arms tighter around his knees. 'I don't think touching you again would be a good idea, Anita.'

'You want to touch me, don't you?'

'More than almost anything, which is exactly why it's a bad idea.' He hugged his knees tighter until I saw the muscles in his arms bulge with the effort. I think he was holding himself tight so he wouldn't give in to the urge to reach out his hand and close the small distance between us.

I sympathized, God knew I did. How many times had I fought against touching Jean-Claude before he finally won that battle? Hell, how many times had I fought not to touch a lot of vampires, or shapeshifters? So many of the preternatural powers grew worse when you touched, but in this moment I needed them to grow worse. They'd taken my weapons, and killing Nicky wouldn't stop Jacob from making that fatal phone call. Without weapons I couldn't kill everyone quick enough to save Micah. I might be able to do something to save two out of three, but at least one phone call would get through. That wasn't an eventuality I was willing to play with, so violence was out for now. I'd put it in reserves for later, but for right now I needed something less violent, and more sneaky. I didn't have a lot of sneaky in my arsenal of skills, but I had a few things. Things that had made Nicky fight his Rex over so little interaction with me. What would happen if I gave him a lot more interaction? What would happen if I used my vampire wiles and tried to take him over? Could I do it? Was I willing to do it? For Micah, yes; for all three of them, hell yes. I'd compromised my moral standards to save strangers' lives, so what would I do to save someone I loved?

There was only one answer to that question: Anything.

I held out my hand. 'Come to me, Nicky.'

'No,' he said, but it was a whisper.

I remembered this game. There'd been a time years ago when I'd fought every time Jean-Claude had wanted to touch me. I'd craved the feel of his hand on my body long before I'd been willing to admit it out loud. I realized with a start that sent jolts of electricity down my fingertips that I wanted to touch Nicky. I wanted the feel of his skin under my hand. Normally, this would have made me run the other way, but not tonight. Tonight I couldn't afford to be afraid of this part of myself, because it was the only weapon I had left.

I thought I'd have to touch him first, but in the end he came to me. He wasn't strong enough to force me to come to him.

He crawled on all fours, closing the small distance between us. Lycanthropes, especially the cat-based ones, can crawl like they have muscles in places no human ever possessed, all liquid grace and sensuality. Nicky just crawled, almost like he wasn't sure it was a good idea. Maybe it wasn't, but when you run out of good ideas, bad ones start to look better.

I expected him to use his hands to touch me, but he rubbed his cheek against the unbruised side of my face. The moment our skin touched the hunger rose inside me in a hot rush of need. I carried Jean-Claude's blood hunger in me, and the hunger for flesh of several wereanimals, and the need in me would have been happy with either. Lucky for what was left of my humanity I had one other option for hungers. The *ardeur* was one of the most specialized abilities of Belle Morte's bloodline, from which Jean-Claude descended. It enabled vampires to feed on sex so they could travel in countries where they were still illegal and not leave a trail of vampire-bite victims behind them. Other bloodlines fed on fear, or anger, and that last one I'd managed to find on my own. I could feed on anger now, but it wasn't as good a feeding and I didn't want Nicky mad at me.

'Oh, my God, what is that?' He breathed it out in a trembling line of fear. His one visible eye was wide, flashing white in the dimness of the shed. The side of his neck was lost in shadows, but I could feel the beat of his pulse on my tongue like candy that I wanted to lick and suck, and finally bite down and let all that rich, hot center burst into my mouth. I leaned forward, aiming for his mouth and a kiss, but that would only be the beginning. His mouth wasn't what I wanted him to open for me. It was a way to get closer to that throbbing heat in the side of his neck. A distant part of me understood that this was wrong, that tearing his throat out would be bad, and my chances of killing him faster than he could kill me were almost nonexistent, but the front of my head was screaming for food. I had planned on using the *ardeur* to roll Nicky and make him help me, but I hadn't planned on the other hungers being this strong. That only happened when I'd used up a lot of energy. Healing used up a lot of energy. How hurt had I been, and how much of my reserves had gone into getting better?

I kissed my way down the side of his face, and then laid my lips against the warmth of his neck. I breathed in the scent of his skin, and it was all mixed together with the trees and the grass, and the distant scent of water on the summer air. He smelled like outside, like the summer had seeped into the pores of his skin and made him sweet and fragrant with its warmth.

Nicky's voice came out hoarse and choked with need. 'Your power is all mixed up with heat and sex.'

My tongue on his neck made him shudder, and something about him doing that while my mouth was so close to the blood pulsing under his skin turned the switch in my head from sex to blood. I fought to move back from his neck and that hot, sweet blood. 'Yes,' I breathed.

'I can feel your hunger now. You want to feed on me.'

'I'm trying for sex here, Nicky.'

'Why isn't my beast rising to yours? Why isn't my hunger rising to yours? Why do I feel like prey?'

They were all excellent questions. It forced me to think, and that helped me push away the urge to feed, enough for me to say, 'I don't know.' The *ardeur* didn't usually turn to bloodlust this easily. Once it was raised it stayed raised, but not tonight. Tonight I had to think myself out of that hot, sweet scent just below his skin. If I tore his throat out, it would be the same as any other violence; it wouldn't save Micah. Jacob would take one look at his dead lion and I'd lose my leopard. That helped me struggle to think about his questions, and how I could turn this craving for meat and blood back into sex. I needed to feed on something, though, which meant that Nathaniel and Damian, at least, knew I was hurt, because of all my metaphysical men I drained them first when I was injured. Silas must have hurt me badly for me to need to feed this much. Jean-Claude had taught Nathaniel and Damian how to feed the *ardeur* and send the energy to me; like any good servant of a vampire, they could feed while I stayed hidden. It was one of the main purposes of having a vampire servant of any kind. But if they'd gathered energy, then it hadn't come to me. If Ellen's barrier could keep out the energy of my leopard to call and my vampire servant, then she was even better than I'd feared. But it meant that until I fed, I really wouldn't be able to raise their zombie; I'd used too much of myself up healing what Silas's blow had done to me. Shit.

I licked over the pulse in his throat. My breath came out in a shuddering line against his skin. I fought not to sink my teeth into his flesh, because I wasn't sure how many times I could resist doing what the inside of my head wanted to do. Eventually, if I couldn't regain more control, I would take blood and flesh, if I couldn't turn this to sex.

He moved in my arms, put his mouth on mine, and kissed

me. The kiss was enough to turn the switch again, and suddenly he was all warm potential in my arms. My hungers didn't care which one got used as long as one of them did.

I heard Jacob's voice yelling outside, 'What the hell are you doing?' I think he was yelling at us.

The door to the shed opened, and Jacob stood there haloed by moonlight, with a second shorter figure in black outline behind him. He pointed the gun at me, but we were so close that it was more like pointed at us.

'Get off her, Nicky.'

I drew Nicky in so that he wrapped his arms around me and lifted me so that we were both kneeling. He leaned in for a kiss, but Jacob was beside us, his anger roiling out like a nearly visible thing. 'Don't you dare.'

I looked up at him, and Nicky began to kiss his way down my face toward my neck. He never looked at Jacob.

'He can't help himself,' the second figure said, and it was a woman's voice; was this Ellen the witch?

'Bullshit.'

Nicky found the bend of my neck and I had trouble concentrating. I moved his face away from me. 'I can't think with you doing that.'

'I don't want you to think.'

'Her power calls to him, as it calls to you, Rex.' Ellen's voice had that distant singsong quality that some psychics get when they're sensing something otherworldly. I realized what she was sensing was me, but for once I couldn't feel it. All I could feel was the weight and warmth of the man above in my arms.

'She doesn't call to me,' Jacob said.

I looked at the other man and I could suddenly feel the connection between the werelion touching me and the one in the doorway. Jacob was their leader, and that meant more in the supernatural community than it did for humans. Jacob had shared his power with Nicky, his beast with Nicky. I knew in that moment that he was the one who had turned Nicky into a werelion. He was Nicky's creator, his alpha and omega, beginning and end.

I had fed on leaders of animal groups before, and knew that through that connection I could feed on all their people at once in a massive feed, but I'd never realized that the reverse might be true – that I could follow the connection between one of the lesser lycanthropes to their leader, and have the control of the lesser help me gain control of the king. But it was there, a tug on my power like a fish caught on a line. It went through me, into Nicky, to his Rex, and through him beyond. Nicky was the key that opened it up, but Jacob was the guardian at the door. If I could take him, I could take them all, including the woman in the door. She wasn't just a witch; she was a lion, too. I felt her beast pulling toward Jacob like a flower moving sunward, but I had power in Jacob now from earlier, and her beast would flow through him, to me. I threw my power outward, searching for how many lions were outside. I touched one more, and he, definitely he, was hurt.

Ellen grabbed at something that hung around her neck, and I couldn't feel her as strongly. She touched Jacob, and I couldn't throw my net of power farther than the doorway.

Jacob aimed his gun at my head; at this distance he wouldn't miss. 'Jacob,' I said, 'you don't want to hurt us.'

The end of his gun began to lower toward the dirt floor. 'I don't want to hurt you,' he repeated.

I felt Ellen's power then, like a red flare behind my eyes. It hurt, and I was suddenly flung back to just sensing Nicky. I couldn't feel Jacob anymore.

'Fuck,' he said, and he took something out of his jacket. 'You hooked up with your vampire master and thought you could roll me like some young kid. I warned you what would happen if you did that.' He was dialing his phone.

I fought panic, and it shut down the *ardeur*, and suddenly Nicky went very still against me. He growled low in his throat and said, 'Now who smells like prey?'

'It's my power,' I said, and knew my voice was thin with fear, but I didn't care. 'I didn't contact anyone outside.'

Jacob was quiet, listening to the phone ring in his ear.

I tried to get up, but Nicky held on to me. 'No,' he said, and I wasn't sure if he meant 'no, don't get up,' or 'no, something else.' But he let me feel just how strong he was as his arms locked around my body. It was like a hug that could suffocate with just a little more pressure. He let me feel the potential in his body for hurting me. There was more than one problem with the *ardeur* shutting down.

'It *is* her power,' Ellen said.

'That's not possible,' Jacob said, and then he frowned down at the phone in his hand. 'Mike isn't answering. It went to voice mail.'

I felt a small spurt of hope. Maybe Micah had figured it out? We had our own bodyguards; maybe Jacob's plan wasn't going so smoothly after all.

'You'd feel if he'd gotten captured,' Nicky said, his arms still locked around me.

Jacob nodded. 'I would.'

'It's her power, my Rex,' Ellen said.

'I thought her vampire powers came through her Master of the City; when you put up the shield against that connection, her powers were supposed to be less.'

'I can only apologize; I didn't understand that some of the powers are her own now.' She dropped to her knees beside him, holding her hand up to him. I'd seen similar gestures among other animal groups. It was a human version of acknowledging that Jacob was dominant to her, and an apology for screwing up.

Jacob stared down at her, and I knew if he didn't take her hand that it meant he didn't forgive her. That could be the beginning of being cast out of your group. He finally lowered his gun hand so she could lay her smaller hand on the back of his; I'd seen much more elaborate versions of this, but apparently Jacob wasn't big on ceremony. It was his pride; he could run it the way he wanted.

'Get her up, let's raise this zombie and finish this,' Jacob said.

Nicky simply stood up with his arms around my waist. There was a moment when he held me completely in his arms, my feet off the ground, and we looked into each other's faces from inches away. He looked disappointed, as if he was worried the *ardeur* had gone, but he sat me down on the ground just the same. But the moment my feet were under me the world swam in streamers of gray and white. I waited for the headache to come back, but it didn't. I was just suddenly so weak. I started to fall and Nicky had to catch me to keep me from falling to my knees. My vision was going in spots and swirls, and I couldn't get my legs to work right.

Nicky changed his grip and I was suddenly being held against his body, while my legs wouldn't support me. I sagged against his bare chest, and the grayness swallowed my vision in little white starbursts, then the world went black and then nothing. There wasn't even time for me to wonder what was happening.

I HEARD VOICES first. A woman said, 'She needs to feed, or she will die.'

'She's human,' a man's voice said.

'Not human enough,' the woman said.

I was lying on my back again, but this time there was something folded under me for a pillow. It took me a moment to realize it was my suit jacket. My bare arms were warm in the summer night. Nicky moved into my line of vision. 'She's awake,' he said. He was sitting beside me, again. It was like a slightly different version of the first time I woke.

Jacob and Ellen came to stand over me. They looked impossibly tall from this angle. Ellen knelt beside me, but kept her hand on whatever she wore around her neck. 'You used a lot of energy healing what Silas did to you, and you're not human, or one of us. You need to feed on energy outside yourself like a vampire.'

I licked my lips and found them dry. I felt impossibly weak, and wasn't sure I could sit up without help. Shit. I found my voice and it sounded thready. 'What is wrong with me?'

'I believe if you do not feed your vampire powers you will die. I did not understand what it would do to you for me to cut you off from all the men you are bound to metaphysically. That was my fault, and I have apologized to my Rex for the oversight, but you are so terribly unique, Anita. How was I to know what you were?'

'It's your job to know,' Jacob said, and his unhappiness was plain in his voice.

Ellen lowered her head, long straight dark hair falling around her face. 'You are right. I did not do my job adequately; I am sorry, Jacob, but if you wish her to raise the dead tonight she must feed first, and I fear it is too late for steaks and human food.'

'What are you suggesting we do?'

'She needs to feed on one of us.'

He glared down at her. 'And who gets to open a vein for her?'

'It's not blood she needs, Jacob,' Ellen said.

He stared down at us for a moment, his gaze going from her to me. 'So it's true, she really is a succubus?'

'You felt her power earlier,' Ellen said; 'you know what she is, we all do.'

'Can I have some water?' I asked.

'Nicky, get her some water,' Jacob said.

'You trust me now?'

'Just do it.'

Nicky got up and went for the open door. I wondered what he'd bring the water back in, but Jacob was kneeling on the other side of me from Ellen, and I had other things to worry about.

'You're our supernatural expert, Ellen. You fucked up, you fix it,' he said.

'What do you mean, fix it?' she asked.

'Let her feed on you.' He gave her an unfriendly look.

'If she feeds on me, then I can't maintain the circle of power that is all that stands between her and the power of her master. If she is this dangerous on her own, imagine what she'd be like with her master's power running through her.'

'Fine, then who do we feed to her?'

Nicky came back at that moment with his hands cupped, water dripping from them, silver in the moonlight. He knelt beside me and looked from one to the other of them. 'A little help here, please.'

Jacob looked at Ellen. She said, 'I'm afraid to touch her for fear what she's done to the two of you will jump to me.'

'She hasn't done anything to me,' Jacob said.

'I am keeping you free of her will by using my will, and my faith.' She opened her hand and flashed a pentagram, then covered it with her hand again.

'The water is leaking out, someone lift her up,' Nicky said, and his voice was impatient.

Jacob made a disgusted sound, but moved closer and put one muscled arm under my shoulders. He lifted me, gently enough, and Nicky put his hands down to me. It was messy, spilling water down my front, but the water was cool and good, and I needed it. When I'd drunk all the water, or had it spilled down me, Nicky took his empty hands and wiped them across my forehead and down my cheeks the way you'd touch someone's face with a cool cloth if they were sick.

I think the gesture surprised Nicky, too, because he sat back from me. 'I don't know why I did that.'

'She's rolled you,' Jacob said, and he started to lay me down on the floor and the suit jacket under my head. He moved away, and I grabbed his wrist. The moment I touched him his pulse sped against my hand and the hunger rose inside me in a wave of heat and need that pulled me up, sitting, and leaning toward him.

He angled in, as if for a kiss, and a pentagram appeared between our faces, dangling on the end of its chain. I half-expected it to glow, but it didn't. Maybe I wasn't quite vampire enough yet. But it let Jacob jerk free of me and go stand near the door.

I looked up at Ellen and her not-glowing pentagram. '*Harm none* is the rule, Ellen; bad witch, no cookie.'

She swallowed hard enough for me to hear it, and backed away from me with the pentagram still bare in her hand. I think she'd thought it would glow, too. Did the fact that it didn't make her wonder if she'd lost some of her faith?

I started to fold back toward the floor, and Nicky caught me, lowering me to the ground. I watched the witch's wide eyes and smelled her fear. 'Threefold law, Ellen; what you do to others comes back threefold.'

She was by the door now. Jacob had walked out while I was scaring his pet witch. 'How do you know that? You're supposed to be Christian,' she said.

'I have friends in your faith. They're good people.'

'Implying that I'm not,' she said, and she was angry now.

I lay there cradled in Nicky's arms and said, 'I'm not implying anything, I'm stating fact. You are a bad witch.'

'You're a bad Christian,' she said.

I laughed, and she flinched. 'God forgives me; how forgiving are the powers you've been praying to lately? You aren't powerful enough to cut me off from all my people without help from something.'

'I am powerful enough.' But her voice was too strident; she didn't believe it.

'Can you smell the lie, Nicky?'

'Yes,' he said, and his voice was thick again. It was almost as if without his Rex there, my hold on him was growing stronger. Was it that, or was it just him touching me?

Jacob appeared in the doorway again. He said, 'You fed on my energy just from touching my arm, didn't you?'

'I think so,' I said.

'Nicky,' he said, 'do you want to feed her?'

'You mean sex?' Nicky asked.

Jacob nodded. Ellen had moved out to stand beside him in the doorway.

Nicky looked down at me, that one eye pale in the moonlight streaming through. 'Oh, yeah.'

'You know it's a bad idea, right?' Jacob asked.

'Yep,' Nicky said.

Jacob nodded. 'Make it quick. We don't have all night.' Then he and Ellen left, closing the door behind them.

Nicky looked down at me and there was something fragile on his face, almost fear, like a child when you close the door at night, but they know the monster is still under the bed. Nicky looked down at me with a knowledge on his face that he was holding the monster in his arms. I'd have comforted him, but it would have been all lies.

The hunger rose in me like a tide that came higher each time I denied it; eventually, if I didn't feed voluntarily, it would choose the method of feeding and one of us might not survive that choice. 'I need to feed,' I said.

'You mean you need to fuck,' he said.

'That'll do,' I said.

He grinned, making his face look younger, more the joker I'd met in the restaurant. Was it only hours ago? 'I'm guy enough to want to do a good job, and it feels good enough to touch you that I want to make sure you enjoy yourself enough to want to do it again.'

I smiled up at him and wasn't sure if it reached my eyes. 'It'll be good.'

'How can you be sure?'

I could have said a lot of things. I could have explained that your inhibitions took the place of a lot of foreplay. Instead I leaned in and kissed his chest where it showed above the overlarge neck of the tank top. The hair was softer than it looked, and like his brown eyes, darker than the blond hair. It didn't mean he wasn't a natural blond, but it made the chances less. There was enough muscle on his chest that I had to work to get a mouthful of meat and bite down.

'Ow,' he said.

'If you don't like teeth and nails then you'll have to protect yourself, because there is going to come a point where I won't remember to behave.'

'Are you saying you'll hurt me?'

I studied his face, tried to see by moonlight if he meant the question. 'Haven't you ever been with another shape-shifter?'

He just shook his head. 'After what happened to his first pride, Jacob forbids it.'

I ran my hand through that silky hair again. 'Oh, Nicky, you are missing so much.'

'After what you've done to us in just one afternoon, I understand Jacob's rule.'

'What have I done to you?'

'Divided us. If Silas hadn't come in when he did, we'd have fought over you.'

I traced the edge of his face under the fall of hair. 'You wouldn't have had to fight if Jacob shared as well as you do.'

'He's our Rex. Kings don't share well.'

'My leopard king does.'

'Leopards aren't lions,' he said.

I pushed him back toward the ground and he let me do it. That was one test passed. I needed to know that he wasn't so dominant that he'd crash my life around all our ears. I raised my skirt up enough so I could straddle him, and the feeling of him hard and ready pressed against me, bowed my spine, and made me shudder above him. God, he was so hard.

His hands found my waist, helped steady me above him. I leaned over him, but the height difference forced me to stop straddling the business end and move up to his waist. I waited to feel the guns at his waistband but it was smooth, nothing there to find.

He answered the question as if he'd felt my hesitation. 'Jacob took the guns after the fight. I don't think he trusts me anymore.'

'I'm sorry,' and I meant it. They were bad guys and they were murderers, but still his life was about to change forever, and you should always apologize if you know you're about to fuck someone's life over.

His hair had fallen back when he went to the ground and I could see all of his face. 'You're beautiful.'

'Isn't that my line?' he asked, and then he turned his head so that his missing eye was more in shadow. I remembered when Asher used to use shadows and his hair to hide from me. I'd broken him of it, convinced him he didn't need to hide anything from me.

I touched Nicky's face, turned him back to look at me full-face. I leaned over and began to kiss his forehead. I covered his face in kisses, one inch at a time. I kissed first one soft eyebrow, then the place where the other eyebrow would have been. He tried to turn away, but I held his face between my hands. He let me lay a gentle kiss on one closed eyelid, then on the soft slickness of the scar tissue on the other side. I kissed my way down his face until I found his lips, and there I stayed longer. I kissed him until his arms came up and held me back. Kissed him until he rolled me over so that he was on top and I was on the floor. But he was too tall for missionary. I needed to see his face, his eye, for this to work.

I pushed at his chest. 'You're too tall! I don't want to stare at your chest the whole time; I want to see your face.'

He laughed. 'You just don't want your ass on the bare ground.'

'That, too, but I need to see your face.'

He rolled to the side and looked at me. 'Why?'

'I want to watch your face while we make love.'

'I don't think Jacob will wait for us to make love.'

'Fine,' I said, 'I want to watch your face while we fuck.'

He made a sound halfway between a laugh and a snort. 'You aren't like any woman I've ever met.'

'You have no idea, Nicky, not yet.'

'Show me,' he said, and he rolled back closer to me.

'Strip,' I said.

'What?'

'When the *ardeur* raises, the clothes will come off. We can either take them off now, or we can rip them off each other and have nothing to wear afterward.'

He frowned at me, looking skeptical, but he went to his knees again and lifted his shirt off in one motion. He looked better out of the shirt than in it.

I glanced away while I started getting out of my clothes. I did not want us to rip up another custom-made holster. I also wanted clothes after we finished. It was not the way I wanted to be naked in front of a man for the first time, but Jacob wouldn't wait all night. I needed to finish this before he came back and checked on us. I needed to finish this before he figured out that I was going to do more than feed off of his lion. Because I had decided that I was going to roll Nicky like any good vampire, except because I wasn't really a vampire, but something else, something more and less. I couldn't use my gaze to make him do what I needed, but I could use the *ardeur* to tie him to me. I could put him in the place that Haven had been trying to get to all these months. I could make him my lion to call.

It was supposed to be an honor, something done with deliberation and care, like a marriage, but I didn't have time for the niceties. It was going to be the metaphysical equivalent of a shotgun wedding. I wanted to ask Micah's and Nathaniel's opinion of it. I wanted Jean-Claude to talk to me first. I wanted my men, but in order to have them alive at the end of the night, I needed help now. That help was nude in the moonlight, and seeing him nude almost made me forget there was a plan. He was beautiful, all that muscle and eagerness painted in stark light and shadow, my moon and stars and darkness. I realized something I hadn't before, the process had already begun. It was about to the point where Haven had stayed. I wanted him, and touching him felt unbelievably good, but I'd kept the Rex out of that last bit of me. It was almost as if by holding the spot open so long I'd left a vacancy sign, and the first new dominant lions I met had both tried to fill it. Shit.

I held my hand out to him. He didn't need any more encouragement. He just came to me, wrapped his hand around mine, and let me lead. For tonight that was nearly perfect.

I opened the *ardeur* and realized that there was a thread of it attached to him already. I even felt another thread out in the night hanging on to Jacob. He was fighting it so hard. There was a small part of me that wanted to force him to come to us, but he didn't share. He would never be able to fit into our lives. He would always have to be king, and I had enough kings in my life. I needed men who were okay with being the power behind the throne, not the ass on it.

Nicky's mouth found my breasts, lifting me in his arms so he could suck them while still on his knees. He sucked and bit until I cried out. Then he let me slide down his body, and I felt him so hard, so eager, that even him brushing against me made me cry out again. He stood up, and it forced that soft, girl sound from me; half startlement and half the feel of his hardness pressed against my body. He sat down with the wall against his back, put his hands on my thighs, and tried to angle me onto him, but in the end I was too impatient for it and wrapped my hand around him. I squeezed just enough for him to make a sound for me, then I guided him between my legs, and he began to push his way inside. The *ardeur* made me wet and ready but only real foreplay made me open.

'So wet, so tight, God!' he said, and his hands let go of my legs and went to my waist, my hips, helping guide me where he wanted me. The sensation of him sliding inside me an inch at a time was the pleasure it always was; there was something about that first entry, that first hard push deep inside me that just did it for me. When he was as deep into me as he could go, so that I felt our bodies wedded as close as they could be, I shuddered around him, my fingers finding the rough of the wood wall that was at his back.

The shudder had thrown my head back. I had to recover enough to look at him. I put my hands on either side of his face at the same time that I began to move in his lap, with him inside me. His hips moved with me, his legs pushing into the ground to give him more movement, and we began to dance together up against the wall in the summer dark.

'Your eyes, they're glowing. Brown and black, like brown glass with light behind them.'

There were other colors he could have said that would have scared me, too, because I'd been possessed by a vampire or two in my day, but he'd described my eyes with power in them. It had only happened a time or two, but it was my power and tonight I needed it. Tonight it didn't frighten me. He stared, mesmerized, into the dark diamonds of my eyes as his body went in and out of mine, and my hips rose and fell with his movements. His rhythm became more frantic, and I ground my hips into him, helped him fuck me as hard and deep as he could. It felt so good, so good, so good.

I breathed his name over and over, as that warm pleasure built deep in my body. 'Nicky, Nicky, Nicky, Nicky, Nicky.' One last thrust and he spilled me over the edge, bowed my spine, and made me scream my orgasm to the sky. But my pleasure didn't let me feed; it was only as his body released inside mine that the *ardeur* fed. And then that was when I truly fucked him. I fucked him in every sense of the word. I fucked him until he brought me screaming again and his body shoved itself one last deep thrust, and the *ardeur* did what it did best, brought him again, made him mine as he cried out my name.

I felt his power, his beast, his essence, his everything offered up in that moment, and the darkest of thoughts came to me. That I could take all he had and leave him dead underneath me in one massive feeding. I fought the urge, because killing him wouldn't help me save the others. Then a thought, not so dark, came – that he could be ours. Ours not just for this moment but for as long as we wanted to keep him. The *ardeur* had accidentally bound men to me before, but I'd never done it on purpose, until now.

I'd meant to make him my lion to call, but in that moment the *ardeur* of the vampire in me understood there was another option, an option that would make him my slave. Animals to call had free will to a point, they had choices. I needed Nicky's choices gone. I needed his choices to truly be mine. I did to Nicky what I'd had vampires do to me when I was just beginning to hunt them. I did to him what I'd seen vampires do to police officers and other executioners. I chose my free will over his. I chose the lives of the men I loved over Nick's freedom. I chose my life over his, and I took him. I took his body, his mind, the heat of his beast, and all the power that gave him. I drank him down through the sweat of his body, the release of him inside me. I drank him down. But there in the dark there was his need. A need to belong, to be held, a need for gentler things than Jacob had ever allowed him. Belle Morte's line deals in sex, love, and power. I was still too new at it to guard myself from the one weakness. We could only control as much as we were willing to be controlled. Only love as much as we were willing to love. Satisfy lust only as much as we were willing to be satisfied. If I had been thinking better, I would have kept to the sex. I knew how to do that now, but I needed him to risk his life for me. I needed him to maybe kill his king, his friend. Men don't do that just for sex, but for love . . . for love people will do terrible things. I needed Nicky to be willing to do anything I asked, and for that I was willing to damn us both.

WHEN IT WAS done, we got dressed. Nicky said, 'Jacob will kill me before he lets me go.'

'We'll cross that bridge when we come to it,' I said.

'I can't love you,' he said.

'Do you mean you aren't capable of loving me, or that you can't possibly love me yet?'

'The second one.'

I held my hand out to him. 'Take my hand, Nicky.'

He put his hand out immediately and took mine. 'I can't refuse you?'

'I don't think so,' I said.

He frowned. 'Why doesn't that scare me? It should scare me.' He sounded afraid, but he kept my hand in his, rubbing his thumb over my knuckles like an idle gesture of long practice. I doubted he even knew he was doing it.

For my part, I didn't just feel healed, or full, but better. I felt energized, as if rolling Nicky so thoroughly had fed the *ardeur* more completely than simple sex. Was this what it felt like to truly embrace the power? Was it just better this way, or was there something about Nicky that made him yummier?

Was this how Jean-Claude felt when he used his powers fully?
I'd ask him when I got home, if I got home. There were still
a lot of problems between me and surviving the night. One
of those problems was striding toward us through the
tombstones.

Jacob's energy rode before him like the promise of lightning
on an edge of storm. 'What the fuck did you do?'

'I fed like we agreed.'

'I felt what you did and it was more than that.' He had a
gun out now, pointed very steadily at me.

'You said you knew what I was, Jacob,' and I felt something
when I said his name. I felt that thread that the *ardeur* had
attached to him pull, as if I could call him by simply saying
his name.

'Jacob, put the gun down.'

He actually started to lower it, and then caught himself.
'Do that again and I will shoot you. We'll eat the second half
of the money before I let you roll us all.'

'Then let me raise Bennington's wife, so we can all go
home.'

'We don't have a home,' Nicky said, 'we have hotel rooms.
Places we rent.'

'We keep moving so we don't have a territory, Nicky, you
know that.'

'We're lions, Jacob, we need a territory. We need a place
to be.'

'You've witched him,' Jacob said.

'You gave him to me for food, Jacob. What did you think
would happen?'

'Not this,' and he sounded pained, as if he took it as a

personal failure that he hadn't understood. 'This is how you have all the men. You feed on them and they're yours. I've seen male vampires do that. Brides they're called.'

'You mean like the Brides of Dracula?' I said.

'Yes,' he said, and the gun was still pointed at me.

'The Grooms of Anita just doesn't have a ring to it, Jacob.'

'No, it doesn't, but Nicky is looking at you like you're his whole world. It's not just sex, is it?'

'No.'

'I should shoot you for this.'

'Jacob, you wanted me well enough to raise the dead. You wanted me to feed on Nicky. You wanted me to have enough power to do what Bennington wants. You wanted to earn the second half of your money, Jacob.'

The gun began to tilt toward the ground again.

'I've done exactly what you wanted, Jacob.'

'Lying bitch.' And the gun came back up, but it wasn't steady now.

'You took his guns after he barely touched me. You and he nearly fought to the death over me, when I'd barely touched either of you. What did you think would happen if you gave him to me to fuck, Jacob? What did you think would happen to Nicky if you gave him to me?'

He rolled his lower lip under, and bit it, I think. 'Fuck,' he said.

'I don't mind, Jacob,' Nicky said, 'it's okay.'

'No, she's right. She barely touches us and we fight. She didn't even kiss you and I didn't trust you with a gun anymore, then I let her fuck you over.' He lowered the gun to point at the ground. 'Raise the zombie, Anita; we'll sort out who's guilty of what later.'

I threaded my way through the gravestones with Nicky still holding my hand. In a way it wasn't just him that had been rolled, because it felt very good to touch him. It had that familiar feel to it, his hand in mine, like an old lover that you'd just found again. It was a lie, but the *ardeur* could make lies seem like truth. It was part of the gift, or part of the curse, depending on how you wanted to look at it. If it got us all out alive, I'd call it a gift, at least until I had to take Nicky home with me, and then I was going to have some explaining to do. *He followed me home, can I keep him?* had never worked for puppies when I was a child, and it seemed totally inadequate for a whole human being.

The grave with the crowd around it was bathed in moonlight distant from the tall trees. Bennington's pale face was turned toward us. Someone was sitting propped against the gravestone, and there was a body crumpled on the other side of the grave. I couldn't see many details, but I'd seen enough bodies by moonlight to know that much.

Ellen was walking toward the grave from farther out in the cemetery. Had she been checking on her circle of power? Did she need to be that close to it to check it? If she couldn't just think and know, then she really wasn't that powerful. Being a werelion should have made her a more powerful psychic, so either she was that insecure or she'd sucked before becoming one of them.

Nicky and I got close enough and the figure sitting by the grave turned and looked at us. I saw the dark hair and the angular face. Silas was too hurt to stand, so why wasn't he at a hospital?

I asked Jacob, who was just behind us. 'Why isn't Silas at a hospital?'

'We can't explain the wound, and we don't want the police involved.'

'That was a silver blade,' I said.

'We figured that out,' he said, and his voice was unhappy enough that I didn't have to know the nuances of it to hear the tone.

'You damn near gutted him, Anita,' Nicky said.

'We'll get him to a doctor, but not until after the job is done.' There was a thread of anger that I didn't quite understand.

'You're punishing Silas, why?'

Ellen answered as she came up on the other side of the grave. 'He overdosed the hooker. He was only supposed to give her enough to make her compliant.'

'What?' I asked.

'He was supposed to get the human sacrifice,' Nicky said.

I stopped walking and turned to see Jacob. I'd forgotten about Silas's errand. How could I have forgotten? 'So some poor working girl gets into Silas's car and never goes home again?'

'Would you rather we pick some random stranger off the street for it?' Jacob asked.

I let go of Nicky's hand and stared at them all. 'What kind of people are you to have agreed to this?'

'She's a meth-addicted hooker. Dying quick and easy tonight is better than what she'll do to herself,' Jacob said.

'Fuck that,' I said, and was up in his face. 'That was not your choice. You had no right.'

'I am the Rex of this pride; I have every right.'

I looked at him, and he met the look, and then dropped his gaze. 'You didn't feel right about this one, and the more you learned the less you liked it.'

'Get out of my head!'

'I'm not in your head, Jacob; I'm looking at your face. It must be a lot of money.'

He glared at me. 'It is.'

'Enough money?' I said.

'Raise the zombie, and we'll find out.'

'Bennington's wrong, you know. I don't need a human sacrifice to raise his wife.'

'He thinks you do.'

'Jacob,' someone said, and it was the first time I'd heard Silas's voice. It was deep to match the size of him. He was more than a head taller than either of the others. 'Why are you talking to her?'

'I am Rex, not you. You don't get to question me, with your mistakes while you're dying on the ground and bleeding out your gut.'

Silas struggled to his feet, using the gravestone to help him stand. Bennington backed away from him with a look of disgust. I wasn't sure if it was the bloody bandages on the front of him or something personal about Silas that he didn't like.

'She's rolled you both.'

'She's rolled Nicky.'

'No, she's rolled you both.' Silas pushed himself away from the grave, one big hand tight to his stomach, just above his belt, as if he were holding something inside.

'How's the stomach ache, Silas?' I asked.

Jacob gave me a look. 'Don't help,' he said.

Bennington said, 'Oh, my God!' We all looked back and found Silas raising a gun. Ellen screamed, 'Silas, no!'

He was pointing it at me as Nicky moved in front to shield me. 'Put it down, Silas,' Jacob said. 'I won't ask twice.'

'She has mind-fucked you both,' Silas said. I couldn't see around Nicky's body, but he was looking behind us, and suddenly we were headed for the ground, him riding me down. Gunshots sounded, and I couldn't see who was shooting. I was trapped under Nicky's body, completely shielded from whatever was happening. The guns were thunderous in the silence. For a second I wasn't sure how many guns had gone off, and then I heard Jacob cursing. 'What the fuck, Silas? What the fuck?'

Nicky rose up enough to look behind us, and then he was on his knees and offering me a hand. 'Are you hurt?' he asked.

I shook my head, and we stood up together, turning toward the grave. Ellen was beside Silas, her face silvered by tears in the moonlight. Her hands were bloody as if she'd tried to stop the wound, but the look on her face said it was too late for that. Jacob knelt beside his fallen man. 'Fuck, fuck, fuck!'

Nicky knelt on the other side of Silas. The three werelions huddled around their fallen man, only Bennington and me left standing, untouched by the tragedy of it all. Jacob pointed the gun at me. 'He's alive, but he won't be for long.'

Nicky stood up and started moving toward me.

'Don't do it, Nicky,' he said.

'It's not her fault, Jacob,' he said, and kept moving toward me.

'Don't shield her!'

'If you want the second half of your money, Mr Leon, she needs to be alive to raise my wife from the dead.'

I think the lions had forgotten about Bennington, or maybe he'd stopped being important. It was his money and his desire that had begun everything, but he was strangely not part of the tableau between Jacob, Nicky, Ellen, and me until he spoke. Then it was as if Jacob remembered why he was there, what had made him risk so much: money.

'The prostitute died while they were screwing,' Bennington said; 'we don't have a human sacrifice.'

'We have something better,' I said, and I looked at Jacob.

'No,' he said.

'You said it yourself: he's dying, and it's his fault the woman is dead. I think it has a nice symmetry to it that Silas is our sacrifice.'

'Symmetry,' Jacob said, and he sounded like he was choking; 'is that what you call this?'

'If you let him die without me raising the dead, then this is all for nothing. You won't even get your money.'

Jacob lowered his gun and nodded. 'Do it, do it before I change my mind.'

Ellen grabbed his arm. 'No, don't let her do this.'

He jerked away from her. 'Can you raise the dead?'

She stared at him with large dark eyes, and just started to cry again.

'Can you?' He screamed it into her face, so that she recoiled from him.

'No,' she yelled back.

'Then shut the fuck up.'

I moved forward, and Nicky moved with me like a big blond shadow. 'What can I do to help?'

'Stay close,' I said, and dropped to my knees on the grave, beside the dying werelion. Jacob looked at me across the body of his man. 'You need to put up a circle of power,' he said, in a voice that was dull with all the shocks of the evening.

'Ellen's put a circle up so wide and deep that I can't feel anything from my vampire master or the men I'm tied to metaphysically. I think her circle will keep out any damn thing.'

'Which means what?' he asked.

'It means give me a blade so I can finish him and raise the dead.' I held my hand out, and he lifted a hunting knife out from under the back of his shirt. It was almost as big as the one they'd taken from me. It gleamed in the bright moonlight, and you just knew it would be sharp.

I looked at the crying woman who was huddled beside the weathered tombstone. 'Can you hold the circle?'

She glared at me, some of the heat of the look ruined by the tears. 'I can hold my end up.'

'Good.'

'You'd better be as good as your reputation,' she said.

I nodded. 'Yeah.' I knelt on the grave, knife in one hand, and grabbed Silas's hair. I bent his neck back, and it was Nicky who said, 'You only bend the neck back in the movies; it's actually easier if you don't hyperextend the tendons.'

I didn't argue, just put the neck back to a more natural angle, and then put the blade against the throat. I dug the tip in and pushed deep as I pulled the blade across his throat. I'd forgotten what kind of power you got from killing a person. I'd only done it once before. And I had forgotten the kind of power you got from killing someone who wasn't a person, but something more than human. I'd only done that once before, too. The power poured over me, through me; my skin vibrated with it, my bones ached with the thrum and beat of all that POWER. Oh, God!

The knife dropped from my hand to the grave, and I dropped to my knees with it. I put my bloody hands on the grave and visualized reaching down through the dirt and pulling her free of it, as if it were water and she were drowning and only I could save her. I screamed her name, 'Ilsa Bennington, rise, come to me, come to me, Ilsa!' The dirt moved under my knees, against my hands. I shoved the power into the grave, into the pieces of body, and there was so much power. I felt her re-form, felt pieces come together that weren't in the grave. The power remade her into something perfect and whole, and that something grabbed my hands through the dirt, and I pulled it from the grave.

She rose blond and dressed in white, her face in perfect makeup. Only her blue eyes were empty, and it took more than power to fill those up. I touched the still-bleeding neck wound on Silas and drew fresh blood across Ilsa Bennington's lips. She blinked, and then a delicate tongue flicked out and licked that blood. She licked her lips, then she blinked again and she was suddenly in there.

She looked at the grave, and at me, and the body, and started to scream. Tony Bennington came and took her from the grave, comforting her, as she asked, 'Why are we here? That's a dead man? Tony, what's happening?'

He walked his dead wife away from the grave, but the power from Silas's death was still there, still in me, and now that the zombie was raised, the power beat through me again. It pulsed through me, hammered along my bones; I'd never felt anything like it. I fell onto the grave, writhing in the pain of it. The power wanted to be used. It was as if my necromancy had become something closer to the beasts inside me, or the *ardeur*, as if the power had a will of its own and that will wanted the dead.

Nicky knelt by me. 'Anita, what's wrong?'

'Too much power from the one death for just one zombie. Too much power for just that.'

'We're in a cemetery; why raise just one?'

I looked up at him, and thought, why not? I got to my knees and put my hands back on the earth and I knew what the power wanted. I knew exactly what to do with it. I put my hands back on the grave and I cast the power down and out. I sent it out and out and out in an ever-widening circle until I touched every grave, every body, and I called, 'Rise, rise to me. Rise!'

Ellen screamed, 'No!' But she was too late, so too late.

The ground moved under our feet, like a small earthquake. The zombies crawled from their graves, but there were hundreds of them and even this much power couldn't bring them back like I'd brought Ilsa Bennington back. These were the shambling, rotting dead, and they pulled themselves free of the earth.

The power hit Ellen's circle and shattered it. I could suddenly feel Jean-Claude and knew that he was closer than two hours away. Every connection I had was suddenly back in place, and I could sense, smell, taste the skins of my men. They were all safe, and some of them were on their way. They'd followed the trail, but now I'd put up a metaphysical bonfire to guide them to me.

But it was Jacob who was yelling, 'You stupid bitch. You didn't just shield her from her people; you cut me off from ours. They were captured hours ago.' He hit Ellen hard enough that her body spun and lay still on the ground. He screamed his rage to the stars.

Ilsa Bennington was having hysterics. Only her husband's soothing voice finally quieted her shrieks. She was screaming, 'Ugly, they're so ugly. Take me home, Tony, take me home!'

Jacob called out to Bennington as he moved through the cemetery of watching dead. 'Bennington, you have your wife just like you asked.'

'I do, she's perfect.'

'Then transfer the rest of the funds.'

'I will once my wife is safely home.'

'Three of my men are captured. One of my men is dead; the other is lost to me, and I just hit Ellen harder than I've ever hit a woman before. Make the damn call now.' There was an edge of a growl in his voice.

Bennington looked offended, but he also looked a little scared. Maybe he was scared of Jacob, or maybe it was the zombies. There was plenty to be scared of in that cemetery. Bennington got a cell phone out of his expensive suit and made the call. 'It should be in your account now.'

Jacob used his own phone to check on that. He nodded. 'It's in the account. Take your wife home.'

They started walking out between the silent watching dead. He was talking to her. 'It's all right, Ilsa. Don't be afraid.'

'You have your money,' I said.

'Yes,' Jacob said.

'She will rot, Jacob. Even with this much power she won't hold together. She can't, because she's a zombie and no matter how good she looks now, it won't last.'

'You're sure of that?'

'Absolutely, and how do you think a man like Tony Bennington will take it when his flirty wife starts to forget she's alive and starts to rot?'

'He'll go to the cops,' Nicky said.

'Or he'll hire someone else expensive to hunt you down, and he'll kill my flirty boys if he can't have his flirty girl.'

'What are you asking me?'

'I'm asking you not to interfere, that's it.'

'What are you going to do?'

'Something symmetrical.'

'Symmetrical,' he said, and then I watched as understanding crossed his face in the moonlight.

'Very,' I said.

He looked past the waiting dead to Bennington and his pretty dead wife. A look came over his face, and he nodded. 'I won't stop you.'

'Stand near me, both of you. Zombies aren't particularly smart.'

Nicky moved close to me, and I offered him my hand. Jacob picked up Ellen's unconscious body and joined us. I spoke to the dead. 'Kill him.'

There was a moment when they all looked at us, a moment when I felt them hesitate, and then I pointed toward Bennington and his blond wife. 'Kill him.' I thought it at them. I pictured his face and I wanted them to move forward, to surround him, and they did.

He yelled, 'Mr Leon, what's happening? What are they doing?'

Jacob called out, 'It's symmetry, Bennington.'

Then Bennington screamed, 'Ilsa, Ilsa, what are you doing! Oh, my God!' The zombies closed around him and began to feed. Bennington shrieked for a long time, and then there were hands reaching for the dead hooker and Silas's body. The sounds were not good sounds. The visuals were graphic. It was like every horror movie you can imagine, but worse. Real bone is always both whiter and wetter. Real blood is darker, thicker, and you don't get the smells on a movie screen. You can always tell when they perforate a bowel by the smell.

One zombie grabbed at Jacob's pants leg. 'Back up,' I said, and it bowed low to the ground, crawling back to the feeding frenzy that had become Silas's body.

I offered Jacob my other hand, and he took it, balancing Ellen's body in his arms. I stood there in the midst of the dead I had raised, and the living they were eating. I stood there holding on to the two werelions, and it was to keep them safer, but it was also because I needed to hold on to something warm and alive. I needed to be reminded that I wasn't just this.

When all the bodies were eaten they turned to me, and I watched, and felt that there was more home in them. There was something in there now that hadn't been there before they tasted flesh. There are things that wait in the dark, that wait for a chance to find a body that they can walk around in, things that were never human. Sometimes you can feel them on the edge of your mind, the shadows that flit out of the corners of your eyes, and aren't there if you look directly at them. The dead that stood there in the moonlight with blood decorating their mouths held the shadows in their eyes. I could finally see what hid just out of sight, just out of thought, and I knew that I could keep the dead. I could keep them animated. They could be the beginning of my own private army. An army of the dead that knew neither pain, nor fear. It would be an army that no bullet would slow, no blade could kill, and only fire would stop.

Nicky squeezed my hand and whispered, 'Something's in there now.'

'Their eyes,' Jacob whispered, 'there's something in their eyes.'

'I see it.'

'What is it?' Nicky asked.

'Shadows,' I said, and then I spoke loud, in that ringing voice that you use in ritual. 'All of you, hear me, go back to your graves. Lie down and be what you were. Rest, and walk no more.'

Their eyes flickered almost like a television that wasn't quite on station, like two channels trying to be on screen at once.

'Tell me you brought salt,' I said, voice low and even.

'Bennington wouldn't let us bring any, because salt is for putting zombies back in their graves and he didn't want you to do that to his wife.'

'Fine,' I said. I knelt, very carefully, keeping my eyes on the zombies the way I did when I was on the judo mat. You never take your eyes off your opponent because if you do they can rush you. I knelt and found the blade I'd dropped into the grave dirt. The blade still had Silas's blood on it. Salt would have been good, but I had steel, and grave dirt, and power. It would be enough, because it would have to be.

I stood up, slowly, deliberately, and called my necromancy. I called it in a way I hadn't before. I called it to use against the shadows in their eyes, the shadows that were promising me power, glory, conquest. *Just let us stay*, it seemed to whisper. *Just let us stay and we will give you the world*. I had a moment to envision a world where the dead truly walked, and moved at my will, but I knew better. I could see it in their eyes. I had animated the dead, but I hadn't filled their eyes with dark power, or had I? Something about them eating human flesh without a circle of power had caused this, and I remembered the third reason for putting up a circle of power before raising the dead. It kept things out. It kept the shadows away.

I'd been arrogant, and I prayed for forgiveness for that particular sin. I was heartily sorry for it. Killing Bennington didn't bother me. 'By steel, blood, and will, I command you to go back to your graves and walk no more.'

There was another moment of that eye flicker.

I put power into the words, all the power I had, and willed it to work. I called the dead to me. I called them with the power that had made my dog rise from the grave when I was fourteen. I called them to me with the power that had put a suicidal professor in my dorm room in college. I called them with that part of me that made vampires hover around me like I was the last light in all the darkness. I called the dead to me, and bade them to rest and walk no more.

I shoved my power into them, and felt something else in

there. Something else that shoved back, but the bodies were too much mine. Too much of my power animated them, and one by one their eyes emptied and they stood like shells waiting for orders.

'Rest and walk no more; by steel, grave, and will, I command thee.' They shambled back to their graves in a silent mass; the only sounds the shuffling of feet and the brush of cloth. Ilsa Bennington came to stand in front of us. She was still the lovely flirt that her husband had been willing to kill for, but her blue eyes were as empty as all the rest. Her mouth was smeared with redder things than lipstick.

Nicky whispered, 'God.' But when I moved to the side of the grave, he and Jacob moved with me. Ilsa lay down on the grave and the dirt flowed over her like water. I'd never had so many zombies lay to rest at once. The dirt made a sound like waves crashing as it covered them all back up.

We stood in a silence so deep I could hear the pulse in my own body thundering in my ears. Then the first night insect called, then a distant frog, then the wind blew through the clearing, and it was as if the world had been holding its breath. We could all breathe again.

'You almost got us eaten alive,' Jacob said.

'You kidnapped me, remember?'

He nodded, and he was pale even by moonlight. Ellen made a small moan in his arms. 'She'll be all right,' he said, as if someone had asked the question.

He looked at the gun that was still in his other hand underneath her body. I watched the thought run through his eyes. 'Don't do it,' I said.

'Why not? You don't have any more zombies to eat me.'

'Jacob,' Nicky said, 'don't.'

'You'll kill me for her, won't you?'

He just nodded.

Jacob looked at me. 'I wish I'd turned down this job.'

'Me, too,' I said.

He looked at Nicky, then back to me. 'They tortured our lions to get this location.' I didn't know who he was saying it to.

'We'd have done the same,' Nicky said.

'You've destroyed my pride,' he said.

'No, Jacob,' I said, 'you destroyed it when you put yourself on the wrong side of me and mine.'

He looked at me then, his eyes so wide there was a flash of white to them. 'I'm going to try to leave before your people get here. Oh, yeah,' he said, 'I feel them like something hot riding closer, so much power coming to your rescue, as if you need rescuing.' He laughed, but not like it was funny.

'Go, Jacob,' Nicky said.

Jacob looked at me. 'If your name ever comes up in connection with another job, I'll turn it down.'

'No matter how much money they offer you?' I asked.

He nodded. 'There isn't a price big enough to get me to come near you again.' He actually looked at the gun in his hand under Ellen's body. I watched him think about it. 'I'll make you a deal, Anita Blake. You don't come near me, and I will leave you the fuck alone.'

'Deal,' I said.

Nicky hugged me. 'I don't think I'm leaving, Jacob.'

'I know that.' He looked at me then, his eyes so wide there was a flash of white to them. 'I wasn't sure if I was going to be able to leave. I'll gather everyone up, and we'll leave you and your men alone. I'd put a sign above St Louis for all the hired thugs, if I could.'

'What would it say?' I asked.

'Here is a bigger motherfucker than you are.'

Jacob returned my weapons and trusted me not to shoot him in the back. He walked to the edge of the cemetery with Ellen in his arms and only when he was about to enter the trees did he turn and look at me. Maybe I should have shot him, but my lioness was content with beating his ass and letting him go. In the world of lions, he wouldn't be back. Here was hoping my lion knew what she was talking about.

THE FIRST HINT of dawn showed above the trees, making them look even blacker against the growing light. I felt Jean-Claude's frustration. He could not come for me, but there were others who could. Others that daylight worked just dandy for, and as if I'd called them just by thinking of them, Micah and Nathaniel came out of the woods with guns, and other dark figures came with them. The cavalry had arrived.

They held me while the other guards made sure there were no more bad guys. They had Nicky at gunpoint, on his knees with his hands behind his head. He looked like he was familiar with the position. I was holding them, and crying, which I never did. 'I thought they'd kill you.'

'When you didn't come back from lunch, Bert called us to see if you'd gone home,' Micah said.

Nathaniel put his forehead against mine. 'Then we couldn't find you, and you missed the call from the other marshal about the vampire execution. We went back to the restaurant you had lunch in and Ahsan, the cute waiter, told us about two men and you getting into an SUV with them.' He began to kiss his way down my face. 'Then you were gone, all our connections to you were broken. I thought you'd died.' He hugged me so tight I could hear the beating of his heart against my body.

I hugged him, and Micah kept my other hand. 'Jean-Claude kept Nathaniel and Damian going with energy, but we knew you were hurt; that much we felt before it all went black.' He came to us both and Nathaniel opened his arms, so we did a group hug.

Jason's voice came. 'I almost die for you and I don't even get a hug?'

I pulled away enough to see him, and he joined the hug. 'Sorry I missed the party but I had to be in charge of finding sunproof housing for the vampires.'

'I felt his frustration that he couldn't get here before dawn.'

'Frustrated is one word for it. Insanely angry is another,' Jason said, and wiped at the tears on my face.

'What do we do with this one?' one of the guards asked.

I turned to look at Nicky, still kneeling at gunpoint. 'He's with me,' I said.

Everyone looked at me. 'I needed help to heal from the injuries, and I needed enough power to raise the dead so they didn't kill you guys. I rolled him. The dead Rex said that he'd seen male vampires that could do what I do; Brides of Dracula.'

'Brides of Anita?' Jason asked.

I shrugged.

'Are you sure you can trust him?' Micah asked, and the look he gave Nicky wasn't friendly.

'I don't know, but I do know that he protected me from his own pride, and almost took a bullet for me.'

'Would you have survived without him?' Micah asked.

I thought about it, and then said, 'No.'

Micah went to Nicky and offered him a hand up. The guards didn't like it, but they knew not to argue with all of us. Micah stared up at the taller man, studying his face. 'Thank you for taking care of her for us.'

'I helped kidnap her, you know,' Nicky said.

Micah nodded. 'I know.'

'Is he coming home with us?' Nathaniel asked.

'I hadn't actually thought that far ahead,' I said.

Then Nicky looked at me, his eyes stricken. 'Don't leave me, Anita. Please, don't leave me.' His face seemed to struggle for an expression, but finally he collapsed to the ground and crawled toward me. He extended one hand. 'Please, please, Anita, I don't understand everything, but the thought of you leaving me behind feels like dying.'

I looked at the other men. Micah nodded. Nathaniel hugged me. Jason said, 'I don't live with you guys, so I don't think I get a vote.'

I hugged him with the arm that wasn't around Nathaniel. 'They threatened to kill you; you get a vote.'

He came to stand with us and looked down at the man with his hand still out. 'Touch him and let us feel the power.' That was Jason, so much smarter than he pretended he was.

I reached out and took Nicky's hand. The moment we touched, the power jumped between us, climbed over my skin in a warm, tingling rush that caressed Nathaniel's skin and crossed to Jason. Nathaniel made a small sound. Jason said, 'Tasty.'

Micah came to us, rubbing his hand up and down the goose

bumps on his arm; the other hand still held the gun. 'You mind-fucked him.'

I nodded. 'Yeah.'

He kissed my cheek. 'I'm sorry you had to do that.' And in that moment I realized that he understood what it had cost me to take Nicky the way I did. I kissed him back and moved into the circle of his arms. I buried my face against the warm scent of his neck and let him hold me. The gun dug into my back a little.

Nathaniel and Jason were helping Nicky to his feet. The bigger man was crying, crying at the thought that I would cast him aside. Fuck.

I looked at Nicky watching me with frightened eyes while Jason tried to comfort him and Nathaniel came to join us, his gun peeking from the side of his jeans and ruining the line of his shirt.

I went to Nathaniel and kissed him, thoroughly and completely, so he melted in against me, our bodies, our hands, pressing against each other. He drew back laughing. 'I love you, Anita.'

'I love you, too.'

'Let's go home.'

I nodded. 'Home sounds great.'

We started walking toward the woods. Jason jogged to catch up with us. I realized that Nicky was still standing back by the grave. I looked at him, so tall, so muscular, and so lost.

'What do I do with him?'

'What do you do with any of us?' Micah asked.

'He's a stranger, and he tried to kill us all.'

'He would do anything you told him to do, Anita,' Jason

said. 'He seems to have even less free will than the rest of us do.'

'I did it on purpose, Jason. I took everything from him on purpose.'

'You did what you had to do, so you could come back to us,' Micah said.

'I really wanted a puppy,' Nathaniel said, 'but I guess we could say he followed us home, too.'

'I told you we'd think about a dog.'

'In the meantime can we take the kitten home?'

'He's not a kitten,' I said.

'He looks like one.'

I looked at Nicky by the grave and knew what he meant. He looked so alone, but he made no move to follow us, as if he'd simply stand there by the grave until I told him to do something else. Had I told him to stay by the grave? I couldn't remember.

'We can't leave him like that,' Micah said.

I sighed. 'Nicky, come on.'

His face lit up as if I'd told him tomorrow was Christmas, and he jogged toward us. We slept in the motel that Jason had settled Jean-Claude and the other vampires into so that dawn didn't find them and do something unfortunate. The four of us shared the king-size bed, and Nicky slept on the floor beside us. He'd started to shake at the thought that he couldn't stay in the same room with me. God help me.

But in the morning, I woke with Nathaniel's vanilla-scented hair across my face, and Micah's warmth pressed against my back. Jason's arm and leg were across Nathaniel's body, touching me even in his sleep. I heard movement on the floor and Nicky sat up, rubbing his face clear of sleep. He smiled at me, as if whatever he saw was the most beautiful thing in the world. I knew that was a lie, but with all my men around me in a warm puppy pile I couldn't be unhappy. I'd taken Nicky's free will; I'd eaten his life on purpose. He could never be free, never be his own person again.

Micah moved against my back and laid a kiss on my shoulder. 'Good morning,' he whispered, and that was enough. Did I regret what I'd done to Nicky? Yes, I did, but as Nathaniel blinked those lavender eyes up at me through a veil of his own hair, Jason mumbled, 'It's too early to be up,' his hand rubbing along my shoulder. I could live with it.

THE END

AFTERWORD

WHERE DO I get my ideas? How do I know if an idea is strong enough to support a whole book? How do I write a whole book? How do I write day to day? What helps me get into the mind-set to pull words out of thin air and write books?

These are some of the questions I get most often from would-be writers or just people who think being a writer must be interesting, or hard, or easy, or just weird. All of that is true, often at the same moment. I love my job. It's all I've ever wanted to do since I was fourteen – well, except for being a wildlife biologist, but that was a fling; my heart has and always will belong to the muse. She hooked me at about age twelve, but she set the hook in hard at fourteen when I read Robert E. Howard's short story collection *Pigeons from Hell*. That was my moment of decision that I not only wanted to be a writer but I also wanted to write horror, dark fantasy, heroic fantasy, to make up worlds that never existed, and write about our world with just a few scary changes. That was my epiphany and I never really looked back.

Flirt is my twenty-ninth novel in about fifteen years of time and space. I know something about writing and about how to treat it like a career. It takes a lot of hard work and a very thick skin so all those early rejections don't crush you. But first you need an idea.

I'll state up front that I don't understand the question, 'Where do you get your ideas?' I had a woman who was raised just across the alley from me ask me after I had several books out, 'How do you come up with ideas like that, when you were raised here?' The implication was that small-town middle of farm country wasn't the most likely place to find a writer of paranormal thrillers. I asked her the question I really wanted to ask, 'How do you *not* come up with ideas like that, when you were raised here?'

I can't remember a time when I wasn't telling myself stories, at least in my own head. I would often tell a true story with just a little embellishment, which is one reason I did not pursue journalism. But most often my ideas were about fairies, monsters, vampires, werewolves – scary but beautiful, or scary but emotionally poignant were always the things that attracted me as a child. I guess I've never really outgrown the idea that if it can drink my blood, eat my flesh, and be attractive at the same time, then I am all over it. By fourteen, I wrote my first complete short story. It was a real bloodbath where only the baby survived to crawl away into the woods. The implication was that she would starve to death or be eaten by wild animals. I was always such a cheerful child.

I have no idea where that first story came from and it wasn't a great idea, but it was the first complete idea and that makes it valuable. But how do I come up with ideas that are book length and good enough to be book length? Funny you should ask that. Because that is exactly what I'm about to try to explain.

I am going to tell you where the idea for *Flirt* first came from. I'm going to tell you the first scene that came into my head, because most books start with a scene for me. I have a little mini-movie in my head or freeze-frame of a visual and that is the peg on which the entire book begins to revolve. That first moment is when I see something or experience something, and I feel that little catch in my stomach, or prickling along my skin. Book ideas are a little bit like falling in love. You're on a date with someone and they do something, or say something, and you get that little uplift where you think, *Yeah, I like this one*. Ideas are like that. I'll tell you the first idea, and I'll even tell you the fertile ground that that idea found to land on, which happened nearly a year before. Because an idea is like a seed; it needs good soil to grow into a nice big book.

I'm going to tell you the schedule I kept, the pages I wrote per day, the music I listened to, and the books that I read for extra research while writing the book. I am going to lay my process bare before you. I'll let you see it from inception to completion. Will this help you do the same? I'm not sure. Will it answer the question of where I got this idea and how I knew it was a book? Oh, yes.

First, what do I mean by fertile ground? I mean a set of circumstances or a mind-set that puts me in a headspace to appreciate the idea and to see almost instantly the possibilities of it. This mind-set has allowed me to write short stories in one glorious muse-driven rush, and this once allowed me to get an idea for a book and weeks later have that book be complete.

It all began with a party at my friends Wendi and Daven's house, which is states away, and that is important to this tale, because it meant Jonathon, my husband, and I had to fly in and stay at a hotel and were there visiting for several days. Among their other lovely and charming guests was Jennie Breeden, who does the web comic 'The Devil's Panties,' which has nothing to do with satanic underwear, but more to do with the semiautobiographical life of Jennie, but funnier. Jonathon and I were fans of her web comic, and we'd met her for the first time at Comic-Con 2007. She turned out to be a fan of my books, so it was a mutual squee-fest. Which was very cool. We met and visited with all of them more at DragonCon the following year, but coming to visit Wendi and Daven was the first chance for me to spend some quality time with Jennie.

I have a lot of friends who are writers. I have friends who are artists from sculpture to woodworking to graphic art and comic books. It's always fun to be with other artsy types. It can help spark ideas and just give you a new perspective, but Jennie's comic is funny. She records, or writes down, funny things that people say around her for later comics. She's doing a daily strip and that takes a lot of funny. I could not possibly do a daily strip. I certainly couldn't be funny every day.

Jennie and I would hear the same thing, or see the same event, but she would then speak into her phone/recorder and it would be funny, even funnier than what happened. I began to help her collect funny bits, but all my ideas sparked by similar things were dark. It was as if we walked through a slightly altered version of the same world. Hers was brighter, happier, even funnier, and there was a lot of genuine funny that trip. My version was darker, more overtly sexual, even aberrant, violent, sometimes violently sexy, and an innocent moment turned into a potential for murder and horror in my head. In Jennie's head, there was a laugh track, and even when the jokes had a sexual flavor to them, they were still charming, and never crossing that line of deviancy that my ideas always seemed to be on the other side of, waving happily at the less debauched across the line. If she had not been speaking out loud into the recorder, or asking us to repeat phrases, I wouldn't have realized how much funnier her version of events were than mine. She also would tweak the reality and it would begin to build into something much funnier.

Later, she contacted me and Jonathon and ran some of the cartoons by us because she didn't want to make us uncomfortable. She takes reality and pushes it to that next absurd level, so that it's not exactly what actually-actually happened, but it's almost what happened. But it was always fun, and funnier for having gone through Jennie's mind and onto the paper.

I realized that here were two artists experiencing the same weekend, but taking entirely different things away from it. It was eye-opening, refreshing, and made me look at things anew. The experience, like much of this last year, helped me lighten up somewhat, but it also confirmed that I would never be truly light and fluffy. It's just not my speed, and at the end of the year I was content with that, happy even with my lighter shade of dark.

Skip ahead a few months, from winter to summer, and Jonathon and I were back visiting Wendi and Daven. It was at the end of the visit and we were catching a late lunch or an early supper (aka 'lupper'), before they drove us to the airport. We were all sitting in a U-shaped booth at a restaurant where we'd gone before with them. It was nice, comfy.

The waiter came to take our orders. He had his little notepad out, pen poised. He asked what we wanted for drinks. I think Jonathon and I ordered first, and then it was Daven's turn; Wendi was on the other side of him. Daven had been studying his menu and only then looked up. I swear, he only looked up and gave the waiter his full face, nothing more. The waiter went from reasonably intelligent, competent, human being to stuttering idiot.

Have I mentioned yet that Daven is six foot three with long, thick hair down to his waist? It's brown, but it's that kind of brown that has natural gold highlights all through it. He has these great big hazel eyes that are truly brown and gray and a little green all at the same time, depending on his mood. He has a Vandyke beard and mustache that he grew so he'd look old enough to date his age group and stop getting hit on by so many men, when all he wanted was to date women. All this is to say that Daven is pretty, very pretty. Oh, and just to add to the treat of it all, his wife, Wendi, is six foot one, blond with huge, soft, blue eyes, and enough curves to make straight men weep and gay women beg. If you are at all insecure about yourself these are not the two people you want to be standing next to.

I knew intellectually that they were pretty, and I knew that

Daven flirted at a black-belt level, but I hadn't until that moment understood the impact he could have simply by looking up. But once Daven realized the reaction, he smiled at the waiter. And the waiter just fell to pieces. I almost felt sorry for him – almost.

The waiter said, 'Um, ah, wh . . . what, I . . .' Out of desperation he sputtered, 'Drinks, I can bring you drinks.'

All four of us nodded in unison, and said, 'Yes, bring us drinks.'

The waiter fled.

Daven turned to Wendi and practically bounced in his seat, almost clapping his hands together in excitement. 'Can I play with him, please?'

'No,' said Wendi.

Pouting, Daven said, 'Why not?' I'm not sure I can explain to you how a man that tall, that broad-shouldered, can bounce in his seat and pout and have it work for him, but he does, and it does.

'Because we'll either get great service, or we'll never get our food,' Wendi said.

The waiter returned with water for all of us, which was great since we all wanted water. He then asked for our food orders. But he took our orders while staring at Daven, as if the rest of us didn't exist. Daven just looked up at him with that beatific smile on his face.

I don't remember why the waiter kept coming back to the table. All I know is we never had to ask for our drinks to be refilled, they just were, and bread never ran out, and, well, the waiter kept coming back and he never looked at anyone except Daven.

Now, I have no problem with both my friends being gorgeous. I usually just enjoy the world's reaction to them, especially to Daven, who just has an aura of charisma that's hard to explain. But I was sitting within inches of Daven. Jonathon and Wendi were at the edges of the U, but I was right there, and the waiter stared at Daven's smiling face. Did I mention yet that I'd asked Daven how he did his charming thing earlier on this trip? I had, and he had explained it to me. It was a technique I would later use to good effect on camera for the commercial and interview for my book *Skin Trade*, but this day, at that moment, I trotted it out for something nearer and more immediate.

I lifted my face up, and because I'm a petite woman, I did the slight head tilt and smiled. The waiter just kept staring at Daven, and I admit that I moved a touch closer to Daven and made certain that the waiter couldn't ignore the fact that I have curves of my own. The only question was, did he only like boys, or did breasts hold some appeal? I waited to see. He did that little eye flick, and then he was dividing his attention between the two of us. I honestly don't think it was that I was flirting that well, but that the waiter had actually realized he hadn't made eye contact with anyone else at the table. He could look at me and still see Daven, because we were beside each other. He couldn't look at either Wendi or Jonathon and still see Daven. My husband is his own share of pretty (shoulder-length waves of strawberry-blond hair), and he grew his own Vandyke beard and mustache that is true orange-red for much the same reason Daven grew his, because he looked twelve and wanted to date his own age group and was tired of fending off more offers from men than women. Cap it with almond-shaped blue eyes like an exotic Viking, and his much cozier size for me (five-eight), and, well, any more description would be oversharing . . . The most important thing I learned about flirting is that it's not just the equipment you have, but how you use it. Daven and I were willing to use what we had on the waiter; our spouses were not willing to stoop to those levels. One must simply tip a hat to the strength of their character, and go back to tormenting the waiter.

We finally got our bill, paid, tipped, and left. The waiter was *sooooo* giving Daven the invitation to leave a number, to call back, to please, don't go. Daven did one more grin and off we went. I believe it was as we were leaving the restaurant that I turned to them all and said the fateful words, 'If Jennie were here she'd turn this into a funny, charming comic strip, but if I ever used it as an idea, it would all go horribly wrong. There would be violence, or violent sex, or both, and a high body count.'

We all laughed, they drove us to the airport, we went home.

But that was the idea, right there.

Fast-forward a couple of weeks and I was deep into the writing of the latest book of my other series, Meredith Gentry, fairie princess and private detective. The book was *Divine Misdemeanors*, and it was kicking my ass. Something was really blocking the inspiration pipeline. Usually that means there's another idea trying to get out. If I can just figure out the idea and write it down then I can go back to the book that's due, and let the idea simmer on the back burner, as it were.

But when I sat down to write this idea out, it didn't stop.

I wrote the first few pages and made myself go back to *Divine Misdemeanors*, but that book slowed to a crawl. I remembered the last time this happened was in the middle of *Danse Macabre*, and the book that came out of that interruption was *Micah*. So I let myself divide my day, working on the book that was due and allowing myself a second writing session on the idea that would not die, and that would eventually become *Flirt*.

How do I divide my attention and my muse between two projects at the same time? Music. I use different music for the different projects so that when I sit down I know by the soundtrack what project I'm into. I find that music can be so intensely paired with a character or a book that I will sometimes have to put that song, or album, or even band, away for a while before I can listen to it again without being thrown back into the book it's so closely associated with. The music for *Flirt* was The Fray, Flaw, and Tori Amos's album *Abnormally Attracted to Sin*. That was the music to sink me into Anita's world and this idea. Over and over for hours, for days, for weeks, this was the music that let my imagination know what we were doing. I find that the right music is like a magic switch in my head and even months later a certain song will make me think of a character, or a scene in my books. I tend to associate real people with songs, too, so I guess the fact that my imaginary friends have their music isn't that surprising, but I find that once I land on the right music, the book, whatever book, writes much better and much smoother. There would come a point where I simply had to give myself over to *Flirt* and let it eat my world for a little bit. Just checked the calendar on my office wall and I actually only let the book have its way with me exclusively for two weeks; the other three months that it lived in my head it had to share its time with Merry and *Divine Misdemeanors*. I averaged eight pages a day, the highest being twenty-five on the last day. It wrote as fast as *Micah* except it took longer for me to be willing to give the book its own time in my schedule. Sometimes working with two different publishers on two different bestselling series is like trying to date two men at the same time. You can do it, but there are moments when each man wants all the attention and there doesn't seem to be enough of this writer to go around. Once *Flirt* was done, I was able to write *Divine Misdemeanors* with a fresh eye, a fresh attitude, and renewed enthusiasm. The same had happened with *Danse Macabre* after *Micah*.

There is a scene in *Flirt* that is based on what happened in the restaurant with Daven and Wendi. I've given most of Daven's part of the event to one of the other men in Anita's life. I gave Micah and Anita Wendi's part. I let Anita do some of my part. I did with that real-life event what Jennie does, except the charming incident would inevitably lead to something going horribly wrong, and there would be sex and violence, and a high body count, just as I'd predicted.

I let Daven and Wendi read the novel early so they could see that I'd done exactly what I said I would do. It amused us all, and I suddenly had a surprise Anita Blake novel for the year. Nifty!

So that was the idea, and that was what it became, and how I wrote it. But to prove to you that it doesn't matter what the idea is, that it matters who the artist is and what they do with the idea, I asked Jennie to create comic strips of the idea. I told her the story of what happened in the restaurant and she did it as a comic. They're funny and charming and no one dies. I managed for the same scene to be funnyish and charming and tender and a little sad, but it would set in motion a series of horrible events, because that's just the way my mind works. And to see how Jennie Breeden's mind works, turn to the comics that follow, and then you will have it all.

Now, how I took the charming restaurant scene and got to a man who wanted his wife raised from the dead at any cost – even the deaths of those Anita held most dear – well, I don't know. Years ago when I had one or two books out, people would guess that I wrote romance or children's books. As a petite woman, I guess they went for the packaging, but as my good friend who is a policeman says, 'Packaging is not indicative of content.' Boy, that's the truth.

I'd tell the people who thought I wrote children's stories, as in picture books, 'No, I write science fiction, fantasy, and horror.'

It was always that last part that got them. I had several people say, 'But you look so nice,' as if you can't be nice and write horror. If asked now, I say, 'I write paranormal thrillers.' That seems to make people happier, and it's more accurate for what I do, since I was mixing vampires and zombies with mystery and romance long before it was a genre of its own. But I still get asked, 'Why do you write about sex and monsters?'

The only honest reply is, 'You say that like I have a

choice. These are the ideas that come to me. These are the ideas that have always come to me. If it can bleed me, eat me, or fuck me, I want to write about it.' Every girl needs a hobby.